TRUTH IN THE LIE

THE LEONIDAS CORPORATION - BOOK 2

TARINA DEATON

TARINA DEATON, LLC

Editor: Jessica Snyder Edits

Cover Design: Lori Loves Books

CHAPTER 1

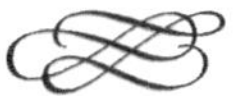

IRAQ

"*Attention on the JOC floor. The time is now zero two hundred hours. This is the current operations briefing.*"

Major Addison Foster clicked on the chat window blinking a new message from her friend Elise.

JOC23 (Elise): Do you have to pay attention to this brief?

HUM04 (Addison): Yes. One of my targets.

JOC23: Boo. Who am I going to kill time w/now?

HUM04: lol. I can still chat. Just need to pay attention to the other windows.

JOC23: Cool.

While the briefing droned on through the mission timeline, communications channels, and weather, Addison checked in to the four chat rooms she monitored during operations—Search and Rescue, Reconnaissance, Current Operations, and the team chat. The last group tended to be the most amusing. She didn't know any of them personally since they were located at a different Forward Operating Base, but she interacted with the analysts enough that she felt like she knew them.

HUM04: Checking in

SOF69 (Team Liaison Officer): Hey. How's it hanging?

HUM04: It doesn't.

SOF69: lol. Never gets old.

"Ten minutes to target."

JOC23: Did you ever hook up w/Petrov?

HUM04: Ew. No. Where did that come from?

JOC23: He just asked me if I wanted to go get coffee at Green Bean. Why ew?

HUM04: He's a man whore, that's why.

JOC23: Maybe that means he can get me to the big Oh

HUM04: Doubtful. Guys like that aren't in it for your gratification. Only theirs.

HUM04: Besides, do you really want his petri dish near your incubator?

JOC23: Ew. And cynical much?

"Five minutes to target."

Addison's stomach fluttered, and she glanced up from her computer screen to the floor-to-ceiling bank of monitors. The close-up black-and-white IR image of the Special Forces team fast-roping from Black Hawks greeted her. The image flickered to the panned-out view to include the compound and all three helicopters.

Her pulse kicked up a notch. Shit. Braedon was on one of the teams. She knew he was in theater, but she hadn't known where since their locations and movements were classified. Even with her top secret clearance, she never knew where her brother was until after the fact.

HUM04: Is Braedon Foster on one of the teams?

SOF69: You know I can't tell you names.

Shit. Shit. Shit. Something was wrong. Her stomach somersaulted the same way it had when he'd fallen off the slide behind their house and broken his arm.

"Three minutes to target."

HUM04: Something is wrong. Call off the mission.

SOF69: What? No. Who is this?

HUM04: Braedon Foster's sister. Something is wrong. CALL OFF THE MISSION!

Her gaze snapped to the big screen. The team was in position, ready to enter the compound.

Her heart thudded in her chest, threatening to burst through her sternum. She looked over her shoulder and up to the top of the theater where the Joint Operations Center, or JOC, commander paced across the walkway.

Pushing back from her chair, she took the stairs two at a time.

"Sir? Sir!"

"What is it?" Colonel Jefferson asked.

"You have to call off the mission," she said.

"What?" He removed the left cam of his headset off his ear.

"You have to stop the mission," she repeated. "Something is wrong."

"What exactly is wrong?"

She shook her head. "I don't know. It's a feeling. I can't explain it—I've never been able to explain it."

"I'm not calling off a mission because you had bad food at the chow hall," he said.

Captain Petrov stepped between her and the commander. "Major, you should go back to your station."

Addison glared at him hard enough that he shifted his weight and looked at Colonel Jefferson over his shoulder.

"You need to listen to the captain, Major, before I have you removed from the floor."

"Ready to breach." This came from the team on the ground.

"Please, sir. I am begging you to call off this mission."

He settled the cam back over his ear and adjusted the microphone near his mouth. "You are a go."

Her stomach plummeted, and only her iron will kept her knees from buckling. She spun and faced the screen. At the bottom of the theater, Elise watched her with worried eyes.

A five-man team breached the compound and hugged the walls around to the back of the main building.

"Team One is set."

The second team set up at the front of the building. Ten seconds later, the first team entered the building from the rear and their heat signatures disappeared. Two minutes after that, the second team entered.

An eternity later, the call out. "Target is clear."

The colonel turned to her and cocked an eyebrow. "See, Major? Nothing to worry about."

No. Something was still wrong. Very wrong. And now she knew for sure. "Get them out of the building. Get them out of the compound."

"It's fine, Major," Captain Petrov said.

"It's *not*. The house should not be empty." The intelligence said the house and compound were a main staging base for ISIS. "Get. Them. Out." Her clenched teeth acted as a barrier to keep her scream inside.

The image on the wall of screens, all twenty of them—half as large as an IMAX screen—exploded in a bright ball of white light. Seconds later, the boom, caught by the mics of the men outside the compound, reverberated through the room.

"The house is gone! Repeat. The house is gone," came the report.

Addison's breath stuttered in her lungs, and she sank to her knees. Chaos erupted around her. The commander shouted orders at someone next to her. Someone entered her field of vision. She could see his mouth moving, but it was as if he was speaking to her underwater. Pushing at him, she stared at the wall of monitors, watching the men still alive run toward the bright flames of the target building. Watched while they got as close as they could. Watched the insurgents racing toward the survivors. Watched the tracer rounds from the close air support strafe the enemy forces. Watched the remaining team sprint for the helicopters that landed to retrieve them.

And she saw none of it.

Her twin—the other half of her whole—was gone.

~

*A*ddison sat in the center of her bed with her legs crossed, picking at her nails. The mission had ended hours ago. She wasn't even sure how she'd made it to her room, vaguely recalling someone leading her. It might have been Elise.

She should feel something. Hollow, maybe? There should be an emptiness yawning wide in place of her heart, but that wasn't what she felt.

There was a knock at the door, then it swung open before she responded. She glanced up as her commander entered. He moved the camp chair from the foot of her bed to in front of her and sat down, resting his arms on his knees and clasping his hands together.

He was an attractive older man, but he looked tired. Older. As a full-bird colonel, he was probably less than ten years older than her. Rank came with its own worries and tonight it showed in the deep lines of his face.

"Major Foster—Addison. We haven't confirmed all the team members or contacted all the family members yet, but I wanted to tell you personally. Your brother was on the mission. He was with the first team that entered the building." He paused. "There were no survivors." He rubbed one hand over his close-cropped hair.

"I understand, sir," she whispered.

"I've got the front office working on getting you on the first transport back to the U.S. You should be home with your family within the next forty-eight hours."

He stood, and she felt the weight of his gaze. He had questions—the same questions everyone always had. How had she known?

Had she always had a connection to her brother? Had it ever happened before? Did he have the same thing?

"We'll do our best to retrieve your brother's remains, but insurgents have overrun the area. It may be some time before we can get back in there and when we do…"

She swallowed hard and nodded. When they did, there would be nothing to find.

"I'm truly sorry, Addison." He left, closing the door softly behind him.

She closed her eyes and concentrated on the feeling deep inside her. It didn't matter if they sent the entire 101st Airborne Division to look for the bodies of the team—her brother wouldn't be there.

He was hurt, but he was alive. Now she needed to figure out how to convince someone to believe her.

CHAPTER 2

ARLINGTON NATIONAL CEMETERY

Addison clenched her fists by her side and dug her nails into the palms of her hands while the honor guard lifted the flag from the gleaming coffin and stepped to the side.

The soldiers at each end snapped the flag tight and folded the corners together, turning the flag with precise, choreographed movements. How many hundreds of times had they done this? Too many, she was sure. And completely unnecessary this time, because her brother was alive.

In the six weeks since she'd returned from Iraq, she'd failed to convince anyone. Not her parents. Not his unit. Not the Navy. No one believed her. They chalked it up to survivor's guilt. Shock or PTSD. An ultimate refusal to accept the truth. She'd even been ordered to undergo a psych evaluation. She'd waited until her request to resign her commission had been accepted before telling her commander to go fuck himself.

The honor guard finished folding the flag and presented it to her mother "on behalf of a grateful nation." Fuck the grateful nation. That same nation was leaving her brother out there somewhere to rot.

One by one, her brother's teammates approached the coffin,

knelt beside it, and pounded their SEAL trident pins into the lid. Each one echoed with a sense of finality that was as devastating as the continued refusal to believe her. They were sealing his fate as surely as if they were pounding nails into his coffin.

Addison couldn't take it anymore. Couldn't watch an empty box be lowered into the ground while the bugler played "Taps" and the honor guard fired the volley. Spinning on her heel on the green carpet laid over the soft ground, she only got a few steps before her uncle grabbed her upper arm and stopped her.

"Where do you think you're going?" he asked in a low voice.

"I'm not staying here for the rest of this farce," she whispered.

"You need to quit being so selfish. Do you understand what this is doing to your parents?"

She glanced to her left. Her mother sat with her head bowed, clutching the folded flag to her chest, tears streaming unchecked down her face, her father's arm wrapped tightly around her shoulders. She knew exactly what it was doing to them. They were too immersed in their own grief to deal with her. She understood and didn't blame them—in their minds, they'd lost their son —but it left her isolated and alone.

Looking back at her uncle, she said, "They wouldn't be going through this if someone would just believe me. He's not dead." She wrenched her arm away and marched off.

Her heels clicked on the wide, paved sidewalk as she left the grass. The signpost ahead pointed toward the Tomb of the Unknown Soldier.

How many families went to the Tomb wondering if their loved one was one of the many unidentified remains interred in the Tomb? How many families spent years coming to terms with the reality they would never know what happened to their missing father, son, brother? How long did it take before they gave up and moved on with their lives?

She couldn't. She wouldn't. She was looking into private investigators, ones with military experience, to help her figure out what happened to Braedon and find him. Finding one that wouldn't feed her a line of bullshit while robbing her blind appeared to be the biggest obstacle.

The hair on the back of her neck prickled and she glanced over her shoulder. A man in a dark suit walked several paces behind her. He'd been at Braedon's sham of a funeral and had been one of the first to pound in a trident. His longish dark hair, combed back from his face, short beard, and lack of uniform said he wasn't active Navy. She'd caught him looking directly at her during the funeral. It could have been because she wasn't sitting with her parents, but she hadn't gotten Judgey McJudgerson vibes off him like some of the other attendees, especially her parents' few country club friends who'd made the trip from Texas.

Looking back again, he was still there. Still keeping pace with her. His relaxed, hands-in-pockets, casual stroll didn't fool her. He held himself the same way Braedon did. Tight and loose at the same time. Like a coiled snake in that moment before it strikes—mesmerizing and deadly.

Addison stopped and turned to face him. "Can I help you?"

*D*evon stopped a few feet from her and shook his head. "Just want to make sure you're safe."

"I can take care of myself," she said.

His lips twitched. "I know you can, Addison."

She cocked her head, and the corners of her eyes tightened. Not quite a full squint, but she telegraphed her distrust well enough.

"Have we met?" she asked.

"No. I'm Devon Nash. I was teammates with your brother." The soft skin of her palm felt like silk in his when she took his outstretched hand.

"You were on the op in Syria with him?"

"No." He shook his head, releasing her hand. "I wasn't there. We served together on our first tour."

"How do you know my name?" she asked.

"Braedon talked about you a lot. He showed me your picture once." A picture Devon had printed out and stuck in his wallet. Faded and worn through at the creases, he'd carried it around for almost a decade—along with his infatuation with his teammate's twin sister.

She nodded and glanced off in the distance before shifting her weight to turn away from him.

He stepped closer, willing her to stay. "I overheard what you said to your uncle. What did you mean when you said Braedon isn't dead?"

Crossing her arms, she dropped her head back before nodding it forward and shaking it. "It doesn't matter."

"It does. Why don't you think he's being buried right now? Other than they never recovered his body."

"Why? So you can tell me I'm delusional or selfish like my uncle did?"

"I have my reasons, but I want to know yours first," he said.

Her eyes jumped back and forth as she searched his face. He didn't know what she was looking for, but she must have found it. "You know we're twins, right?"

He nodded.

"Braedon and I have always shared a connection. When we were babies, if one of us was sick, the other one threw up. It made doctor's visits hell on our mom. We always knew when the other was hurt or hurting. I knew he was on that mission and I knew something was wrong." She swiped her fingers under her eye, catching the tear before it could fall. "I know he's not dead because I would feel it. Instead, I feel him. He's not dead, but he's not okay either. And no one will do anything about it because no one believes me. Everyone thinks I'm overcome with grief and in denial, so I've convinced myself he's alive."

Addison shook her head, pressing her lips together.

Devon took another step closer and touched her elbow. "I believe you."

"Why?"

Up close, he could see the lighter flecks in her blue eyes. "The company I work for was contacted regarding one of the other men on the op and we came across information about your brother. I can't share it with you here. Can you make it to Charleston next week?"

Two small lines formed between her brows. "South Carolina?"

"Yes."

"I guess," she said.

Releasing her elbow, he pulled out his wallet and took out a business card, handing it to her. "Here's the address and my contact number. If you can be there Monday, I'll set up a meeting with the head of the company at zero nine hundred. Does that work?"

She looked down at the card and back at him. "Yes."

He nodded and returned his wallet to his back pocket. "I promise I'm not trying to be cryptic on purpose. I think it would be better for you to get all the information at once, and I was only told the basics on the drive up here yesterday."

"Okay."

"Would you like some company while you walk?" he asked.

"No, thank you. I need some time alone."

"All right. Call if you need anything before Monday." He shoved his hands in his pockets to keep them to himself instead of pulling her into his arms and telling her everything would be okay. He couldn't make that promise just yet, and she probably wouldn't appreciate the gesture from a complete stranger. He turned to leave, only getting a couple of steps.

"Devon?"

He turned back around, ignoring the pulse low in his groin at hearing her say his name. She still held his business card in both hands. "Yes?"

"Would you have told me about Braedon if you hadn't overheard me?"

"The plan was to contact your parents. After hearing your uncle's response, I thought it best to speak to you first."

"Are you still going to speak to my parents?"

"I can, if you think that's best."

She shook her head. "No. I'll—I don't think telling them right now would accomplish anything."

"I'll leave that up to you," he said.

"Thanks." She turned and continued on the path toward the Tomb.

CHAPTER 3

*A*ddison pulled her truck into a spot in front of the nondescript two-story building and shifted into park. This appeared to be the right place, at least according to the GPS. She wasn't sure what she was expecting, but an old office building in the middle of an overgrown parking lot near the docks wasn't it.

She glanced at the dash clock, then back at the front of the building. She wasn't that early for her nine o'clock appointment, but there were no other cars in the parking lot. Maybe the employees parked in back and had a separate entrance?

The Leonidas Corporation. Addison huffed out a short laugh. Either someone was a serious military history buff or they'd watched the movie *300* one too many times. Not that she hadn't—especially that scene with Gerard Butler's butt on display.

She'd suspected from the name of the company that the owner had been in Special Forces. A quick internet search had confirmed her suspicions. It made sense. Most of them viewed themselves as modern-day Spartans—vanguards and defenders of freedom.

Who knew...maybe these guys were. She dropped her head

against the headrest. Maybe she'd become too cynical and disillusioned over the course of too many deployments and no resolution to the problems of the world. It was hard to hold on to hope when the most important person in her life was missing.

She picked up the business card from the center console.

Devon Nash.

Shivers prickled along her spine. She'd racked her brain trying to remember if Braedon had ever mentioned him but kept drawing a blank. Not that it meant anything—Braedon had mentioned a lot of his teammates in passing, usually by call-sign, and other than the few he'd dragged home for random Christmases because their families were too far away, Addison had never met any of them.

Still, something about him was...familiar. Her reaction at Arlington had been visceral. Like a rubber band pulled too tight, waiting to snap back and yank them together, she'd felt incomprehensibly drawn to him. It had taken all her self-preservation not to ask him to hold her. If he'd offered, she would have curled up into him and sobbed out all her worries into his shoulder.

That reaction more than anything had her guard up. She was not that woman—the damsel in distress who needed all her problems taken care of by the big strong man. She did not damsel.

The dash clock showed 8:52 and there were still no other cars in the parking lot. Turning off the ignition, she threw her phone into her purse and hopped down. That was a lot easier to do in her normal boots than today's wedges.

Clicking the key fob to lock the doors out of habit more than anything else, she approached the glass double doors, pushing through them into the empty vestibule. Another set of glass double doors led into an open foyer where a large security desk stood.

"Hi. My name is Addison Foster. I have a nine o'clock appointment," she said.

The guard, an older man who bore a striking resemblance to Sam Elliott, flipped over a magazine and stood, holding out his hand.

"Aiden Graham."

His rough palm enveloped hers, his index finger resting against the inside of her wrist.

Retired Special Forces—she'd bet another five dollars.

She cocked her head. "I'm meeting with Aiden Graham," she said. "But I don't think you're him."

"My son. Aiden Graham Junior. I'm Senior." He walked around the desk and gestured to the corridor to her right. "I was apparently annoying everyone by hanging around doing nothing, so they put me on the payroll."

"How long have you been retired?"

"Longer than I was not retired, but I like to be in the thick of things." He gave her a sheepish smile. "So, Junior put me to work in the hopes of keeping me out of his hair."

"Does it work?" she asked.

"It might. If he had any hair."

Addison chuckled at his response. "Are you security or receptionist?"

"I fill in where I'm needed. Down in the range. Backfill for security every now and then. Today I'm filling in as receptionist since another one quit, and the temp agency doesn't have anyone to fill the position. Or so they say."

She felt like there was more to the story but didn't have a chance to ask as they entered a large open office space. Again, not what she expected.

Except for the area toward the back littered with computer equipment, the entire area was open. Not a cubicle to be found. Instead it was a hodge-podge of desks and workstations.

"Don't mind the mess," Aiden Senior said. "We're still moving in and setting up."

"How long have you been in the building?" she asked.

"The sale was finalized a few months ago, but some of the reconstruction took a little longer than expected. Junior's office is back here."

She'd missed the office tucked into the far back corner of the space.

The senior Graham rapped twice on the door and pushed it open. "Nine o'clock's here."

Addison stepped into the office. Aiden Graham Junior stood from behind his desk and approached with his hand outstretched. She had to tilt her head back as he came close. A few inches taller than his father, he almost towered over her. But it was more than his height. She was used to being around men who exuded constrained energy, but Aiden took it to a whole other level. His presence took up physical space as if his body was too small to contain all of him.

"Thank you for coming on such short notice, Major Foster," he said.

"Of course. I just hope the trip won't be in vain," she said.

"I don't think that will be the case at all." He looked at his father. "Dad, since you're going to hover around anyway, can you get everyone over to the conference room?"

The two men held a stare-off, left eyebrows cocked in an almost identical expression of challenge. Aiden's lifted slightly higher, and his father's lips twitched.

"On it," Senior said with a nod.

Once his back was turned, Aiden closed his eyes and rubbed his forehead, mumbling something under his breath Addison didn't catch.

"Would you like something to drink, Major Foster? Coffee or water?" he asked.

"I could use another coffee. Addison is fine."

He nodded. "Let's see if there's some fresh coffee in the kitchen. And call me Graham."

"Doesn't that get confusing with your father also being Aiden Graham?"

"Not usually. Everyone calls him Senior. The only time we run into issues is when someone calls and asks for Mr. Graham." He turned a corner and walked through an open doorway into a fully equipped kitchen.

Two men crowded around a petite Latina woman. She stood facing them, arms out in a protective gesture, a fierce and angry look on her face.

"What's going on?" Graham asked.

"Tell them to back off, Graham." The woman kept her focus on the men as if they were velociraptors and she was Chris Pratt.

"We just want some coffee, Ange," the man on the right said.

"You can have it when it's finished brewing," she said. "And after I get my cup."

The guy on the left groaned dramatically. "That's going to take forever. I need caffeine now."

"Then you should have fixed the pot yourself instead of waiting for me to fix it," the woman said.

The second man took a small step closer. "But you make it best, Angie. That's why we ask you to do it."

Her eyes narrowed to slits. "Bullshit. You ask me to make it because you're a lazy, entitled, chauvinist a—"

"Angela," Graham said, a stern warning in his voice. "We have a client." He looked at Addison out of the corner of his eye. "Sorry about this."

The corners of her mouth tugged up. She hadn't heard any true animosity in Angela's voice. It reminded Addison of fighting with her brother more than anything. "No problem."

Angela, defender of caffeine and feminism, shifted her now wide-eyed gaze to them. She dropped her arms and stood up straight as the two men turned.

"Oh. Oh! You're Major Foster. I'm so sorry for...them." She waved her hand in front of the men. "And that you had to see this."

Addison smiled. "That's okay."

"It's just that they try to pour coffee before the entire carafe is full, and it messes with the strength and taste of the coffee," Angela said.

"I understand completely," Addison said.

"I'm Angie." She took a step forward before realizing her mistake.

"No!" She spun and lunged at the counter, but one of the men caught her around the waist and hefted her under his arm.

"Don't ruin the brew!" She flailed at the coffee pot while the man not holding her pulled the carafe from the hot plate and poured coffee into a cup.

Graham released a long-suffering sigh while Addison failed to stop the soft laugh that escaped. It might have been the first time she'd laughed honestly in weeks.

"Conference room in ten minutes," Graham said. "Bring Major Foster and me cups of coffee. *After* it's finished brewing."

Shaking his head, Graham gestured for Addison to return the way they came. "I'm sorry about that. I promise you my people are very good at their jobs, despite their juvenile behavior just now."

She stopped in the corridor and faced him. "Don't. Their behavior, juvenile or not, tells me more about your company and you than I can get from your website. That"—she pointed toward the break room—"tells me your people trust you enough to be who they are. I'd rather see that than a bunch of stiff suits with too much composure and bearing."

She swallowed hard before softening her voice. "I'd rather see empathy in someone's eyes when they realize who I am instead of dollar signs, which is all I've seen so far."

He glanced toward the break room and the faint sounds of laughter. "Thank you. I worked for a few companies before starting TLC and I didn't want to run a company like any of the ones I worked for." He cocked his head back toward the main area. "Still, I promise you, we are all very good at what we do."

"I asked around about you—I wouldn't be here if I didn't already know that."

"That's good to know," he said.

"What's good to know?"

Addison turned toward the voice. Whoa. In contrast to the khakis or jeans and polos with the company logo everyone else wore, the woman coming down the hall screamed bombshell in a knee-length black skirt, sky-blue blouse, and four-inch platform heels. Combined with the black-framed glasses, the woman gave off a sexy librarian/dominatrix vibe that made Addison question her sexuality the same way Ruby Rose did.

By comparison, Addison's peep-toe wedges, fitted slacks, and wrap blouse, which she'd thought understated and professional, were dowdy. Ruby Rose wouldn't give her a second look with this woman around.

"That Addison heard good things about us when she asked around," Graham said. "Addison, this is Paige Davis, Chief Operations Officer for Leonidas. Truthfully, this company wouldn't be nearly as successful as it is if it wasn't for her. She runs things while I get to run around the ass-end of the world and still play soldier."

Paige shook Addison's outstretched hand. "It's good to meet you. I'm sorry it had to be under these circumstances."

"Me too," Addison said.

"Paige, can you take Addison to the conference room while I round up the children? They're arguing over coffee again," Graham said.

"Sure. Grab me a cup while you're in there if Angie will let you near the pot."

"Ha." Graham walked back to the break room, leaving her with Paige.

"I'm sure he already apologized for whatever they were getting up to," Paige said as they continued down the hall.

"He did. I assured him there was no need. It's nice to see a group of people comfortable enough at work to be who they really are."

Paige opened a door at the end of the hall, revealing a room with the requisite long conference table and the largest T.V. Addison had ever seen.

"Wow, that's a big screen."

"Right?" Paige asked. "I suggested a standard projection screen. You would have thought I said we should get a black chalkboard and do math calculations with an abacus the way Angie reacted. I will admit it's great when we do movie night, but don't tell her I said that."

Addison smiled at her conspiratorial tone. What was it about this group of people that had her smiling and laughing more than she had in the past two months?

Voices carried down the hall, and Graham and the three people from the coffee conflict filed into the room.

Angie carried a tray with cups of coffee. "I didn't know how you liked your coffee, so I brought sugar and creamer," she said.

"Black is fine," Addison said, accepting one of the mugs.

"We're waiting on a couple more people and then we'll get started," Graham said. "Sorry for the delay—there was an accident on the bridge and they got stuck behind it."

Butterflies took flight in her stomach as she recalled exactly why she was there. They had information on Braedon. They'd been able to distract her for the last half hour, something that rarely happened, but now her fingers began to tingle as her nerves set in.

A tall, well-built, and tattooed man sauntered into the room. "Sorry we're late. Bridge. Accident. Stopped to help."

"I know," Graham said. "Devon called."

Devon strode in behind the first man and managed to suck all the air out of the room. That was the only explanation Addison had for why she was suddenly breathless. His blue-gray eyes bore into hers when their gazes met, and she fought not to look away. The intensity of his stare felt like a physical caress as he searched her face.

"All right," Graham said. "Let's get started."

CHAPTER 4

"Dad, you want to join us instead of lurking around the corner?" Graham asked.

Addison looked down at the table to hide her smile.

"I was just passing by to get some coffee," the elder Graham said.

"Uh-huh. Grab a seat," Graham said.

Graham Senior sat in the seat closest to the door and slouched down, folding his hands over his stomach. He caught Addison watching him and winked.

Graham ran a hand across the top of his head. "Let me start with proper introductions. You've met Paige. Angie Rodriguez, who you met briefly earlier, is our IT, cyber, and network specialist. Turner Breslin is our pilot. Jeremy Owens is weapons and locksmith. Christian Knight is our master mechanic, and Devon, who you met last week, is one of our personal security specialists. We have a few more guys who are currently on assignment that we may pull in depending on what's required."

Addison said hello to the two men who'd been in the break room, the man who'd entered ahead of Devon, then Devon.

"Angie?" Paige prompted.

"Right." The petite woman picked up a wireless keyboard and her fingers flew across the keys.

The large screen flickered to life with service pictures of Braedon and one of his teammates, Michael Drake. Addison blinked hard, unwilling to let the tears fall.

"About two weeks ago, the family of Michael Drake received a phone call from someone claiming to be Michael telling them he was alive," Angie said. "Jonathan, Michael's father, thought it was a scammer or troll trying to get money out from them by pretending to be Michael. Until the person on the line said, 'Tell Nana I want a peanut butter and mayonnaise sandwich when I visit.'"

"What's the significance of that?" Addison asked.

"Michael's grandmother made it for him when he was a kid," Paige said. "He hated them."

"The line went dead before Mr. Drake could ask for more information," Angie said.

"Did they report the call?" Addison asked.

Graham nodded. "They contacted the local police who said it was probably a scammer. They tried the Navy, who fed them the same line. Eventually they got ahold of us."

"Any idea how he was able to call?" Addison asked.

Paige shook her head. "None."

"I served with Jonathan's uncle," Graham Senior said. "I asked Junior to look into it."

Addison caught more than one short-lived smirk at the name Junior.

"With the Drakes' permission, I was able to trace the call," Angie said. A satellite map of eastern Europe and southern Ukraine appeared on the screen.

"It originated from a coastal location on the Crimean Peninsula. Once I had a general location, I dug some more and was able to find proof of life for Michael Drake." She paused and licked her lips. "And Braedon Foster."

She clicked a key on her keyboard, and two more pictures popped up.

Addison inhaled sharply, tears springing to her eyes. The picture on the left was grainy, but it was Braedon. His bottom lip was swollen and bruised, as was one eye, and lacerations dotted his face, but the set of his mouth and fury in his one visible eye was unmistakable.

"When was this taken? Where is he? Why hasn't anyone notified the Pentagon?"

"Based on the pictures' metadata, they were uploaded about two weeks ago—around the time the Drakes received the phone call," Angie said.

"We haven't notified anyone because, by the time the cogs of the big government wheel get going, it will be too late," Graham added. "If we go public with this information, they'll disappear, and we may not be able to find them again."

Addison tore her gaze from the picture. "Why?"

Graham looked at Angie, who clutched the keyboard to her chest. "I found the information on Michael Drake and your brother on the dark web. It led me down a really ugly, super-dark rabbit hole of human trafficking—men sold in auction for their perceived genetic superiority."

"You mean sex trafficking?" Addison asked.

"Um...I think so. Most likely. Yes." Angie winced.

Taking pity on her, Paige continued, "Two U.S. Special Operations personnel would be an extremely rare commodity. As far as we've been able to learn, your brother and Michael are being held by an organization called The Cooperative."

Addison licked her lips. "The Navy reported five members of the team were killed. What about the other three?"

"There's no chatter on them. Either they're being auctioned at another time or they're..." Angie's voice broke at the end.

"Dead," Addison whispered.

"Yeah."

Addison's gaze flitted around the table, stopping on Devon's. His gaze was intense—fierce, protective, and determined. At that moment, it was too much to handle with everything else she was feeling.

She pressed her lips together and pushed her folded hands against her forehead. She didn't know what was worse—knowing her brother was alive and being held captive by a black-market slave ring or being told he was dead. A small part of her wished he were dead. At least then she'd know for sure. Know he wasn't in pain or scared or hurting. This…this was horrible. She pulled her bottom lip into her mouth to keep it from trembling. This was worse than she could ever imagine.

~

*S*itting two seats down the table from Addison, Devon watched her process the information that her brother was alive and being held captive. Everyone at the table remained quiet, even Angie, whose ADHD usually resulted in her talking to fill the silence. She still shifted from foot to foot, pain and empathy etched on her face, but she stayed quiet.

The urge to push back from the table and gather Addison in his arms was almost overwhelming. It wasn't his right or his place and she didn't seem the type to accept such overt, public comfort. Not from a virtual stranger anyway.

Knowing that didn't help tamp down the rage burning inside him. His palms itched to touch her—had itched to touch her since the moment he'd walked into the conference room. A strand of hair had fallen at her temple, and he wanted nothing more than to cradle her head, push that lock of hair away from her temple, and tell her it would be okay. Take all the hurt and pain she desperately tried to hide and promise her he would make it okay. They were going to help her and get her brother back—whatever it took.

Addison rubbed her hands against her forehead twice before lowering them to the table. Her cheeks puffed out as she blew out a breath before sipping her coffee.

"So, they're in Crimea?" she asked.

"We believe so, yes," Graham said softly.

"How did they get there from Syria?"

"We're not sure how the events in Syria played out, but they were probably moved overland to the Black Sea," Paige said. "Crimea is a hotbed for black market activity."

"If the military isn't going to help, what about the State Department?" Addison asked.

Graham shook his head. "They have no presence in Crimea and they're prohibited from traveling there, so there's no help on that front."

"Then what?" Her voice caught at the end, and Devon clenched his jaw, watching her struggle to stay calm. "What good is knowing he's alive if there's no way to get him?"

Searching the room as if looking for an escape, or a lifeline, her gaze found his. If he could only touch her, but he wasn't close enough. All he could do was convey his support through his gaze and provide a stable anchor.

Paige did what Devon couldn't—wrapped her hand around Addison's. "We're going to get him, Addison—him and Michael."

"We who?" she asked.

Finally, Devon had something to give her—a promise he swore not to break, no matter the cost. "Us. TLC. We're going to get him."

CHAPTER 5

Addison shut the door to her room and leaned against it for several seconds before shuffling to the bed and flopping facedown. She was exhausted. Mentally. Physically. Emotionally. Despite that, she was keyed up—wound so tight she might explode at any second. She needed some calm.

Rolling over, she stared up at the underside of the blue chintz-patterned canopy. That matched the blue chintz bedspread and pillow shams. And the blue chintz wallpaper. And the upholstered chair. Anything that wasn't blue chintz was tatted lace. The bed-and-breakfast on Queen Street was in the heart of historic Charleston, only blocks from downtown and more affordable than the chain hotels nearby, but the décor was...over the top. There was no way she was going to find any calm in the midst of it.

Lifting one leg at a time, she unbuckled the straps of her wedges, flipping them off onto the floor. So what if they weren't red-soled, black patent leather, four-inch, platform heels? They were cute and comfortable and suited her.

Pulling her phone from the inside pocket of her purse, she

searched for yoga studios around her. The third link down pointed to a daily yoga session in the Battery. Addison checked the time on her phone—she had almost forty minutes before the class started. More than enough time to change and walk there.

In less than ten minutes, she had her yoga mat slung over her shoulder by the stretching strap she used to carry it and headed down the stairs to the foyer, fighting the urge to slide down the gleaming wood banister à la Mary Poppins every step of the way. She ran her hand over the polished wood and spotted Mrs. Little, the owner, sifting through envelopes at the desk. Maybe the day she checked out, after she'd paid the bill. That way she couldn't kick her out.

"Headin' anywhere excitin'?" Mrs. Little asked.

Addison stopped at the base of the stairs. "I found a yoga class in the Battery."

"I remember when I was bendy. Good for you. There's a nice café on the way back, on King Street, about two blocks north of the Battery." In her soft, southern accent, it sounded like "Bat-tree."

Being from Texas, Addison had worked hard to lose her drawl during college, but she would totally rock a southern accent if she could. How long would she have to live in the South before she developed one? Hopefully not as long as the Littles.

During her tour of the house, Mrs. Little had explained her family was new to Charleston, having only moved there in the nineteen-twenties. Apparently, anyone who hadn't been living in the city when Sherman set fire to Atlanta was nothing but an interfering carpetbagger.

"Thanks, I'll check it out on my way back," Addison said.

"Enjoy your class."

Addison pushed through the screen door to the covered porch, and it struck her again how idyllic the house was. Overflowing flower baskets hung across the front of the porch between white columns. A tall live oak provided shade for most of the side yard, where a large fountain trickled a steady stream of water over the lip of the upper basin.

It was picture perfect, and she wanted to smash it all into jagged little pieces.

Leaving through the wrought iron gate, she turned left before crossing at the corner and followed King Street south, dodging around clusters of people who obviously had nowhere pressing to be, judging by their meandering pace.

Her phone vibrated against her thigh, and she pulled it out of the slim pocket of her yoga pants. Wincing, she pressed the green button and put the phone to her ear.

"Hey, Mom."

"Hi, honey." She sounded weary. Not just tired, but worn down, dejected—all the words that could be used to describe a mother coping with the loss of her only son.

Addison's heart ached to tell her mother the truth. To give her some sense of hope that Braedon was alive, but she couldn't handle the same argument they'd been having since her return from Iraq, even though she now had proof.

"Where are you?" her mother asked.

"I'm in Charleston," she said.

"West Virginia?"

"South Carolina, Mom."

"Oh. What are you doing there?"

"A friend invited me to visit for a few days."

"That sounds nice." Her mom sounded distracted. "When are you coming home?"

Addison stopped at the corner, waiting for the light to change, and rubbed the center of her forehead. "I don't know, Mom. I need to figure some things out. I'm going to look into a potential job with some companies my friend recommended."

She hated lying to her mom, but she also didn't want to tell her the truth. She couldn't go home—especially not now. She couldn't be around them as they wallowed in the loss of Braedon while she knew he was alive.

"We really need you home, Addison," her mom whispered.

Swallowing hard, she said, "I know, Mom. I just need a few weeks. I'll be home soon, I promise. How's Dad?"

"He's keeping busy. He and your uncle Steven have been going out on the boat almost every afternoon."

"He's not drinking, is he?"

"Addison…"

He was. Son of a bitch. She hated her uncle. Never mind his judgmental ass at Braedon's service—she refused to call it a funeral anymore—he enabled her father, a life-long functioning alcoholic who'd been sober for more than a decade. She stopped walking and moved closer to the building so she was out of every-one's way.

"Mom, I know this is hard. I know more than anyone how hard this is, but do not make excuses for him. He needs to get his ass to an AA meeting before I get home, or it will not be pretty."

"He's suffering, Addison."

"So are you. So am I. That does not excuse him drinking again."

Her mother's sigh was heavy as it came through the phone. "He needs time, just like you do."

"Mom—" Her voice broke, and she squeezed her eyes to hold back the tears. "I won't do this again. I won't."

"I'll talk to him tonight when he comes home," she promised.

"He needs to stay away from Uncle Steve," Addison said.

"He doesn't have anyone else to confide in."

"Who the hell are you?" she asked. "He should be confiding in you. He should be confiding in a grief counselor. He should be confiding in his sponsor. He should not be confiding in the guy that provides him with a case of beer every day."

"We all deal with loss in our own way, Addison. Some of us bury it, and some of us deny it."

Her spine went rigid at her mother's dig. "I have to go."

"Addison—"

"I'll call you when I know I'm heading home." She ended the call and slid her phone back into her pocket. She needed some peace and Nama-fucking-ste.

She reached the park and headed to the farthest corner where the website said the class would be. Assuming the twenty or so people with yoga mats were what she was looking for, she approached the woman standing in front, facing the group.

"Hi. Is this the Harmony Yoga class?" she asked.

"Hi. Yes. I'm Crystal. Did you sign up online?" the woman asked.

"I'm Addison." Her shoulders sagged. "I didn't. Was I supposed to?"

"No, not at all. I just didn't want to charge you if you'd already paid online. The class is five dollars."

"Of course." Addison pulled out the bills she'd shoved into the pocket with her phone and ID and handed over a five.

"Do you need a receipt?" Crystal asked.

"No, I'm good."

Crystal smiled brightly. "Great. Find a spot where you'll feel comfortable. Please make sure your cell phone and any other electronics are set to silent, and we'll begin in a few minutes."

"Thanks." Addison walked around the group and chose a spot toward the back and side. She could see Crystal but wasn't in the thick of the group. She smiled at a few people who glanced at her, then unrolled her mat, kicked off her shoes, and dropped her phone, money, and ID on the grass in front of her mat.

"Welcome, everyone." The small portable speaker next to Crystal amplified her voice enough that Addison could hear her clearly from where she was. "I'm so glad to see several new faces along with so many regulars. If you'll take a seat on your mat, either cross-legged or in lotus position, we'll begin."

Addison sat and crossed her feet over her legs, resting her hands palms up on her knees and splaying her fingers before allowing them to relax.

"Let's begin by linking our breaths with our motion. Bring your arms up and out to the sides as you inhale deeply, then bring them down through heart center as you exhale."

She moved through the poses, trying to follow Crystal's soft voice. Tried to focus on her breathing and clear her mind, but even as her body moved from one pose to the next, her mind and spirit refused to quiet. Instead it was as if each new pose released another tumbler on the lock that held her together. The more tumblers that unlocked, the weaker her hold became until her control slipped through her fingers.

Thankful they had moved into pigeon pose, she rested her forehead on her hands as the tears splashed to the mat under her. She barely contained the sob that racked her body, but she stiffened when a soft hand rested on her back.

"Addison, why don't you move to child's pose," Crystal said softly next to her head.

She nodded and pulled her outstretched leg under her, resting her butt on her calves. She cradled her face in her hands and let go. Shame joined fear, anger, and worry in their efforts to overwhelm her.

This wasn't her. She didn't lose control. Or...it hadn't been her. Nothing had been the same since that compound exploded. It hurt too much to keep fighting. Until today, she had been close to accepting what everyone else had said—she was in denial and so desperate for Braedon to be alive that she latched on to the connection of their youth as a reason to believe he hadn't been killed.

Relief, too, coursed through her. Relief that he was alive and she wasn't crazy. She could face whatever came next, knowing he was alive.

A whine and a wet tongue licking her cheek made her raise her head. Which gave the small, floppy-eared dog the opening it needed as it bathed her chin and neck. Addison pushed up and swung her legs around, crossing them in front of her, and wiped her face with the collar of her shirt.

"Hey there, little guy." She picked him up and looked between his legs. "Girl. Where did you come from?"

"I don't know, she just ran over and made a beeline for you."

Addison glanced away from the puppy to find Crystal sitting on a mat close to her. They were the only ones there, the rest of the class having dispersed. How long had she been curled up on herself?

"Hey. Sorry about…that. I hope it didn't disrupt the class."

"Not at all. A few people asked if you were okay, but I assured them I'd sit with you until you were ready."

Addison nodded and rubbed her face against the puppy's side. "Thank you. And again, I'm sorry, I don't know what happened."

"Don't apologize. One of the things I love about yoga is that it causes us to be honest with ourselves. With our bodies, our minds, and our spirits. You were obviously in a place where you needed to release some bad energy." Crystal tilted her head. "Is there anything I can help with? I know I'm a complete stranger, but I'm a really good listener."

She clutched the puppy to her chest. "I…uh. I lost my brother recently, and it's been hard."

"Would you like to get some coffee and talk about him?"

She appreciated that Crystal didn't offer her empty platitudes or sympathies. She was so tired of hearing, "I'm so sorry for your loss." Crystal didn't even ask if she wanted to talk about it—about his death or her loss—she asked if Addison wanted to talk about him.

Oddly, she did. She wanted to tell someone about her brother who hadn't known him as a SEAL or a military hero. She wanted to share all the silly fights they'd had growing up and the time she'd busted him making out with his first real date.

"Yeah, I would." She ruffled the puppy's floppy ears. "We should see if we can find her owner first."

Devon paced in the foyer of TLC, waiting for Addison to arrive. He'd stopped at her hotel the night before to see if she wanted to get dinner, but the older woman at the desk had told him Addison was out. No where. No with whom. No idea when she'd return, just that she'd left carrying a yoga mat. He wasn't sure if she really didn't know or if she didn't want to tell a strange man where her female guest had gone.

There were six yoga studios in downtown Charleston, and he'd thought about going by every single one to find her. He managed to stuff his crazy down long enough to realize there was no guarantee she'd even gone to a studio, and wandering around Charleston looking for a woman carrying a yoga mat was over-the-top psycho. Figuring a yoga class couldn't be more than an hour, he'd asked if it would be okay for him to wait for her return. The woman told him to knock himself out, so he had.

For two hours. Then another twenty minutes, because he appeared to have masochistic tendencies, before finally giving up and leaving.

Graham had sent out a group text for an eight a.m. meeting,

which Addison had been part of, so here he waited. The longer he waited, the more amped up he became.

"Son, you're going to wear a hole in that tile, if you don't calm down."

Devon glanced at Graham Senior, sitting behind the huge reception and security desk, sipping coffee from a mug that read, "Every Day I'm Sparkling."

"'Bout time for a mustache trim, isn't it?" he asked.

Senior lowered his mug and brushed the edge of his mustache with his hand. "If I trim it, I can't filter out the grounds of my coffee, now can I?"

He shook his head. "How come you didn't give any hair to Aiden?"

"You'll have to talk to his mama about that." He ran a hand through his thick, gray hair. "Her daddy's as bald as a newborn. Aiden'd have some hair if he didn't shave it so close."

"Yeah, but then he'd look like George Costanza," Devon said.

"Who's that? New recruit?"

Before he could explain the character reference, the front door swung open and Addison strolled through, a tote bag slung over one arm and a to-go coffee cup in the other hand. "Morning."

"Where were you last night?" he asked. It sounded harsh even to his own ears.

Judging by the way her eyes widened and then narrowed, it sounded harsh to her, too. "Excuse me?"

"I stopped by to see how you were doing and whether you wanted to go to dinner, but you weren't there," he said.

"I went to yoga."

"For three hours?"

She shifted her weight, placing it all on one leg, which cocked out a nicely rounded hip. "I went for coffee with the instructor after dinner. Is there a problem?"

He knew—*knew*—he shouldn't answer that question, but he was apparently too intent on digging this hole. "We need to have our heads in the game, not be going on dates with yoga instructors."

Her eyebrows rose, and she pursed her lips, shooting a look at Senior before turning back to him. "Well, *she* realized I was upset and offered me a sympathetic shoulder. I didn't realize making friends and having coffee wasn't allowed. I'll make sure it doesn't happen again."

She strode past him, her long legs eating up the distance, before disappearing down the hall.

"Damn it," he muttered, running his hands through his hair. He deserved the attitude she'd thrown him.

"You're not a bright one, are you?" Senior asked.

Devon sent him a self-deprecating look. "Not one of my best moments."

"That the way you meant it to go?"

"Of course not."

"Better go fix it." Senior pointed toward the hall with his coffee mug.

"Yeah." Fuck, he was a dumbass.

Jogging down the hall, he turned the corner just as Addison turned into the conference room. "Shit," he muttered.

He slowed and walked in right behind her. "Addison," he said.

"Oh my God! Is that a puppy?" Angie pushed around Jeremy and rushed toward Addison, her hands outstretched, her focus on the large tote hooked over Addison's elbow.

Angie pulled the small dog from the bag and raised it above her head before cuddling it close. "You are so precious! Where did you get her?"

He'd been so intent on sticking his foot in his mouth he hadn't even noticed the dog's head sticking out of Addison's bag.

"She found me in the park yesterday during yoga. I tried looking for her owner, but no one claimed her, and the vet I took her to couldn't find a microchip. I didn't want to take her to the pound, but I'm not sure what to do with her."

Angie's eyes widened. "I'll take her!"

Addison shook her head. "I can't ask you to do that."

"You're not asking—I'm offering. I've been thinking about getting a dog for a while, but all the ones I've found have been big dogs and I can't have a big dog in my apartment, and she's so tiny. Just look at her."

He loved Ange like a sister, even though she scared him sometimes with how smart she was, but her timing was shit. The meeting wasn't for another five minutes. He needed those five minutes to fix his fuck-up.

Angie pressed kisses to the puppy's ear. "Do you know what kind of dog she is?"

"The vet thinks beagle mix. Maybe chihuahua," Addison said. "He said she shouldn't get very large and that I could bring her back if I had to."

"No!" Angie pressed the puppy's head to her chest. "You can't take her back! She's Leonidas now. We don't give people back." She turned back to the puppy. "No, we don't. You're one of us now. Yes, you are. Yes, you are."

"Angela, what are you doing?"

They all turned to find Graham and Paige behind them.

"Isn't she precious? I'm going to name her Princess. My sweet, precious Princess."

Graham ran a hand down his face and through his beard. "You're cleaning up after her. Can we get started?"

"Oh! Right! Yeah." Angie handed the dog back to Addison and moved to the computer at the front of the room, shaking the mouse to wake up the computer.

Devon waited until Addison took a seat then sat in the one next to her, farther away from Angie and the screen. That way he could look at her without making it too obvious.

"Okay. I spent a lot of time on the dark web last night. Way more time than I ever want to spend there, for the record, but I found the information for the auction," Angie said. "It's happening eight days from today."

"Where?" Addison asked. "How do we stop it?"

"We…can't," Angie said. "The auction is invite-only, and even then, it's pay-to-play. Fifty thousand dollars, just to RSVP in the affirmative. No other information is passed until the money is paid."

Devon could only see Addison's profile, but he saw her eyes close and the small shake of her head.

"Even if I cashed out my retirement fund, I don't have that much money sitting around," she said.

"TLC will cover it. Along with the cost of operation," Graham said.

Devon sucked in a breath between his teeth. That wasn't chump change. Even with the extremely lucrative contract TLC had recently been awarded, the company would take a hit.

"I can't let you do that," Addison said.

"The Drakes put down a retainer when they hired us to find their son. It's not going to cover the entire cost, but it covers a good portion of it," Paige said.

"Then I'll match their retainer," Addison said. "It's only fair— we're getting Braedon out along with their son, so I'll pay whatever they're paying."

Paige and Graham exchanged glances. "All right," Paige said. "I'll draw up a contract, and we'll go over it this afternoon."

Addison nodded. "Okay."

"There's still the issue of it being invite-only," Angie said, wringing her hands and wincing. "I can't find anything on what format the invite is in to recreate it."

"Think Shady can get us an invite?" Graham asked Paige.

"I'll call her as soon as we're done here."

"What else do you know about the auction?" Devon asked.

"It's women buyers only. Men can attend as companions, but only women can bid during the auction, and they're only allowed to bring one male companion for either security or…other things. I found a couple of discussions about who was taking who in what capacity." Angie paused and grimaced. "There were pictures. I need eye bleach."

"The women-only thing is going to be an issue if we're able to get someone on the inside," Paige said. "I'm going to need more than one person as backup."

"What about Dani?" Devon asked.

Paige shook her head. "She's training for a fight and is out for the next two months."

Damn. Dani, their resident mixed martial artist and combatives instructor, would have been perfect.

"You don't have any other women working for you?" Addison asked.

Huh. Devon had never considered the lack of women in Leonidas. Maybe because Paige was always front and center, he never saw it as an issue.

Their COO shook her head. "We have a few who work in corporate security, but none of them have the necessary training or experience for something like this." She turned in her seat to glare at Graham. "Which is one reason I want to recruit more women."

"We'll discuss that issue later. Right now, we need to figure out who's going with you."

"Me," Addison said.

"That's probably not a good idea," Graham said.

Devon agreed—silently. He'd at least learned that lesson. It was a bad idea to have family members on ops with each other, especially when the op was to rescue one of those family members.

"Why?" Addison leaned forward and rested her forearms on the table. "I have the training. I have the experience. And this is *my* brother."

Paige and Graham had one of their silent conversations he'd grown to recognize. Watching them, anyone would think they were a couple, but as far as he knew, they'd never been together. Not even back in the day before TLC. All he knew was they went through some shit together when they'd been deployed to Iraq, and it'd made them tight.

Hell, he knew that truth—he had guys he'd drop everything for in a heartbeat. It was a short list, but Braedon was one of those guys. Devon wouldn't have made it through selection if it hadn't been for him.

They finally ended their silent discussion. "How long are you on leave?" Graham asked.

Addison leaned back in her chair and rubbed the sleeping puppy's ears. "I'm on terminal. I resigned my commission."

"Really?" Paige asked.

"It was that or be court-martialed for telling a two-star to go fuck himself."

"Yeah, that'd do it," Jeremy said.

Graham drummed his fingers on the table. "Who're we sending with her? We're going to need Turner on standby. Mac's slated for that personal protection detail next week. Harrison's too young. That leaves Tinker, Jane, and Cactus."

"Who?" Addison asked.

"Sorry," Graham said. "Bad habit of using call-signs—Christian, Jeremy, and Devon." He nodded at Jeremy and Devon.

Before he could even suggest either of the other two, Devon said, "We need Jeremy and Christian on extraction, especially if we have to procure transportation and weapons locally. So it's me —I'll partner with Addison."

He leaned forward on the table, and she turned his way enough he could see her face. "Braedon's my friend," he said softly. "I want him out of that hellhole and home as much as you do."

Her gaze met his. Maybe not as much, but he'd do anything to make it happen. Whatever she found in his gaze was enough, because she tilted her chin in agreement.

"Devon, take her down to the armory and get her kitted out," Graham said. "We need to take as much gear with us as we can."

"I'll call Connie and see if she can help us," Paige said. "Angie, once we get the invitation, you need to work your magic and find us everything on the location—physical and electronic security, interior and exterior, ingress and egress. If you can find schematics of the location, even better."

Angie nodded sharply. "On it."

Paige looked at Addison. "When was the last time you weapons qualified?"

"Nine months ago," she said.

"Jeremy, set her up to shoot while she's downstairs."

"Copy."

Devon glared in response to Jeremy's smirk. He knew exactly where his train of thought was headed, and he'd be damned if he got anywhere near Addison.

"Addison, come back upstairs when you're finished and we'll go over the contract."

CHAPTER 7

"So, Addison, any plans for dinner?" Jeremy asked as they waited for the elevator.

Devon glared at him over the top of her head. The asshole grinned in response.

"Yes, actually," she said.

His gaze snapped to her. What? How the hell could she have dinner plans?

"Only in town for a day and you've already got a date. Nice," Jeremy said.

Fucker.

"It's not a date," she said. "Just dinner with friends."

The door opened with a ding, and she stepped into the car. Devon took the brief opportunity to punch Jeremy in the arm. Hard.

"Ow."

Addison turned in the elevator and faced them, brows raised. "Am I going by myself?"

"No." Devon stepped in and stood close on her right side, edging her toward the wall so Jeremy was forced to stand next to him. He leaned over and muttered, "Keep it up and I'll tell Angie you switched out her coffee for generic."

"Asshole," Jeremy said out of the side of his mouth.

Devon smirked and pushed the button for the basement. "Just get the range ready."

Addison leaned forward at the waist and took them both in. Her brows pinched, and she got a look on her face like she was trapped in an elevator with a couple of crazy people then she leaned back slowly, watching them out of the corner of her eye.

The doors opened, and Devon shoved Jeremy ahead of him before gesturing for Addison to precede him. "We're going left."

She stepped to the left and waited for him. He led her down the short hallway to the equipment room.

"What all's down here?" she asked.

"Underground garage, a gym, a couple of sleeping pods, the equipment room, and at the other end of the hall is a five-lane indoor range and armory."

"Wow. I never would have suspected all that was in here from the outside."

He held the door for her as she entered. "When Graham bought the building, the only thing down here was the parking garage—he added the rest."

"His dad said there was a delay in the renovation," she said.

"Yeah. The range took longer to get certified than expected." He led her through the locker room, where everyone stored their personal gear, to the storeroom where they kept replacements. "What size vest do you wear?"

"Small," she said.

He took a vest from the shelf and handed it to her before grabbing the ballistic plates and inserts. Turning back around, he froze, gaping at the scene before him.

Addison, in the process of removing her blouse over her head, bared the smallest sliver of skin above the waistband of her slacks, revealing the soft curve of her stomach and the small jewel nestled in her belly button.

His mouth went dry as the July wind in Kuwait, and he brushed a hand over his mouth. Fuck. He wanted to flick that tiny rhinestone with his tongue and find where that tattoo on her shoulder disappeared to under her tank top.

"What?" she asked, catching him staring.

"I wasn't expecting to find you half-naked." Thankfully, his cargo pants were relaxed so his raging hard-on wasn't glaringly obvious.

She pulled down the hem of the tight undershirt, adjusting it over the waist of her pants. "I'm not naked—it's a camisole. I didn't want to wrinkle my blouse when I put the vest on."

Taking the plates from him, she dropped the vest to the floor and inserted them like she did it every day. Considering she'd been deployed a couple of months ago, she might have. She stood and slid the vest over her head, bouncing and shrugging her shoulders to settle the weight. After pulling the side bands closed, she stretched her neck from side to side.

"Can you adjust the straps in the back? It needs to be tighter." She turned and faced the opposite wall.

Stepping behind her, he pulled on the tabs on the back of the vest. This close, he could smell her perfume. Something light and floral. She had a small birthmark on her nape, just under her hairline, shaped like an upside-down heart.

"A little tighter." She glanced over her shoulder.

He flinched, caught staring at the nape of her neck. "Sure." He pulled on the tabs, studiously blocking out all the little details he noticed about her until she told him it was tight enough.

"Do you want to shoot in the vest or without it?" he asked.

"Without, if I have the choice," she said.

"Without it is."

Addison ripped open the large Velcro tabs with a loud *kriiitch*, did the same with the inner elastic support band, and slid the vest over her head. It caught the clip in her hair, causing it to tumble around her shoulders in waves.

His palms actually itched to touch it.

Handing him the vest, she gathered her hair in her hands and twisted it, securing it to the top of her head.

He was so fucked. It was karma. Whatever wrongs he'd done in a past life were coming back to torture him now.

Shaking his head, he set the vest on the workbench and grabbed magazine pouches and a combat first aid kit from the rack.

"I'll do that," she said. "I like them a certain way."

"Of course." He stepped back while she organized her kit and watched the play of arm muscles as she worked. It wasn't even like he'd never seen her bare arms before. Or legs.

"Do you want a T-shirt to wear while you're shooting?"

"No, I'm good. Thanks, though."

Right. *She* was good. Devon adjusted the crotch of his pants, now that she couldn't see him. *He* was not.

Leaning against the shelving, he finally had the perfect vantage point to check her out at his leisure. The last picture he'd seen of her had been from around five years ago. She didn't normally blog except when she was deployed. In one of her posts, she said it was one of the few ways she stayed sane, but she'd posted about a girls' weekend to the Florida Keys. She'd included a few pictures of her in a bikini, and he was guy enough to admit he saved them for his spank bank.

His gaze traveled from her shoulders, dotted with freckles, down her back and waist, over the gentle swell of her hips and ass. She didn't have a full-on hourglass figure, but she dipped and swayed in all the right places. He knew from her beach pictures she was toned, but not to the point she lost any of her softness. The shoes she wore, putting her a few inches shy of his own six foot one, did awesome things for her ass.

He shifted his gaze up when she picked up the vest and turned.

"Where should I put this?" she asked.

Grabbing a black go bag from the shelf behind him, he said, "Keep it in here for now. I'll come back later to tag it and put in any equipment you might need."

She slid the vest into the bag and pushed it back on the workbench toward the wall.

"I'm sorry about this morning," he said. "I was out of line."

She braced her hands on the edge of the bench behind her, which thrust out her breasts.

Do not look below her chin.

"Why did you?"

He should have expected her to dig for info instead of gracefully accepting his apology. Dropping his head, he ran a hand around the back of his neck, searching for an answer that wouldn't give him away as a stalker with a decade-long infatuation.

Stick to the truth. At least some of it. "I was worried. And frustrated. I owe Braedon a lot. I wouldn't be here today if it weren't for him sticking his neck out for me. I feel...responsible for you."

"The only one responsible for me, is me," she said firmly.

"I know that intellectually, but it's not going to stop my gut from feeling that way."

She crossed her arms at her waist and tilted her head. "I think I have some antacid in my purse."

He grinned at her response. One of the reasons he'd followed her blog, other than the occasional picture, was her sharp wit and humor. "I'll give that a try when we get back upstairs. Ready to shoot?"

"Yeah." A softness entered her eyes, and her shoulders relaxed a fraction of an inch, releasing some of the tension she'd been holding.

That tight spot between his shoulders relaxed in response. "This way."

He led her down the hall, past the elevator, and waved his wallet in front of the badge reader, unlocking the door.

"That's the first time I've seen anyone use a badge," she said.

"We have to use them to enter and exit the garage. Graham and Paige were adamant about the security of the armory and range."

"Welcome to my inner sanctum," Jeremy said, arms outstretched. "I've got you set up on lane five. M4 and M9 are already at the station."

"Do you have a twenty-two?" she asked.

Jeremy placed a hand over his heart and staggered back. "Do I… Do I have a twenty-two?"

Devon rolled his eyes. "Really, Jane?"

"Why do they call you Jane?" Addison asked.

"You ever see the show *Firefly*?" Devon asked.

"Yes. Oh! Jane! You like guns. Got it."

"All right. Twenty-twos. I've got Smith and Wesson, Ruger, or a Sig Sauer," Jeremy said.

"Let me try the Ruger," she said.

"Perfect choice." He turned and unlocked the cabinet behind him, pulling out the handgun and held it out grip first. "Here you go."

"Thanks."

He grabbed a box of ammo and three magazines. "No problem. You need any help sighting?"

Devon took the box and magazines and placed a hand in the center of Jeremy's chest. "I've got it covered, Jane."

He smirked. "Sure thing.

Devon glared and caught Addison's amused look, before badging her through the holding area into the lanes and flipping the light to indicate the range was hot. He wasn't kidding when he'd said Graham had been adamant about security. TLC's range was more secure than some commercial firing ranges.

The guns were laid out on the counter along with eye and

hearing protection, and the paper target was already clipped to the board.

"You want to shoot pistol or rifle first?" he asked.

"Pistol." She loaded ammunition into one magazine, while he loaded the other.

He pushed the button to send the target to the end of the lane, stopping about three-quarters of the way down. Rolling a foam earplug, he said, "Whenever you're ready," then stuck the plugs in his ears while she did the same.

Devon took note of everything—her posture, her stance, her grip—all as a professional courtesy, of course. She hesitated on the first shot but quickly went through one magazine before dropping it and slamming in a second. In a little more than a minute, she'd expended all thirty rounds.

Taking the headphones off her head, she glanced up at him from the corner of her eye while he brought the target back in.

"Nice. This is probably your first shot." He pointed to the one hole left of center on the target. All the other shots were clustered at the head, torso, and slightly lower. He shifted in sympathy for his paper friend.

"Yeah. No matter how often I shoot, I always screw up the first one."

He replaced the paper target with a new one and sent it back down the lane.

Addison locked and loaded the M4 rifle and adjusted her stance before glancing down and flicking a cartridge away with the toe of her shoe.

"Do you want a different pair of shoes?"

She shook her head. "I'm good."

She was shooting in heels and a camisole and looked like a sexy badass served up on a spent brass platter. Karma was determined to make him her bitch.

At his nod, she flipped the selector to semi and fired off three rounds. He pulled in the target to see where they'd landed.

"Three up, two left," he said, indicating how she should fix her sights, then sent the target back while she made the adjustment.

They repeated the process twice more, but after each adjustment, her shots were still slightly off.

"I'm not sure what the problem is," he said. "You're making the proper adjustments, and I can't see anything wrong with your stance or your breathing."

"Ugh. I know what the issue is. Send it back." She switched her grip and settled the butt of the rifle against her left shoulder.

"Are you ambidextrous?" he asked.

She looked over the stock. "No. I'm left-eye dominant."

"Why not just shoot left-handed from the beginning then?"

"I'm always hopeful I'll be able to sight on my right hand. I'm more accurate with my left but I'm not as fast."

Sure enough, the next three shots were dead center of mass. Sending a clean target down the lane, he couldn't hold his concern in any longer.

"Addison, I'm going to cross a line again."

She lowered the muzzle of the rifle slightly and gave him her attention.

He held her gaze for several moments, debating whether it was worth it. He knew what her answer was, but he couldn't hold back. "I don't think you should go on this mission. It's *not* because I don't think you're capable," he said before she could respond. "It's because I think you're too close to this, and too much emotion, the wrong kind of emotion, can lead to mistakes."

If her gaze could have set him on fire, he'd be a pile of ash at her feet. Maybe rightly so, but he wouldn't be any kind of team leader if he didn't voice his concerns. He didn't want to see her get hurt—and not just physically. They had no idea in what kind of shape Braedon would be. If she flinched at the wrong time, it could affect them all.

"I haven't spent the last forty-eight days trying to get someone to believe that Braedon is alive only to sit on the sidelines and wring my hands like a poor little lady, waiting on word that he's all right. Someone took him and is hurting him, and I will do whatever I have to do to help get him back."

She settled the rifle against her shoulder, flipped the selector to auto, and tore a hole in the target.

CHAPTER 8

Half an hour later, Addison still seethed as they rode up the elevator in silence, unsure why Devon's suggestion bothered her so much. Other than the inherent misogyny associated with his comment. It wasn't as if it was the first time someone attempted to sideline her because she had enlarged mammary glands and a vagina, but it was the first time it truly angered her. The first time she took it personally and not as rote sexism.

Maybe because, for a moment after he'd apologized for his morning blunder, she'd felt a connection. He'd done his best to apologize for his actions and he'd meant it. More than that, she'd thought there was another reason for his outburst other than feeling responsible for her. She...liked him. Yes, he was attractive, but there was more to it than looks.

That edge that all special forces guys seemed to have was tempered by a softness she caught hints of every now and then. It didn't blunt the edge—it honed it. Made it less jagged. Possibly more lethal.

Then he'd told her she should sit this one out. While she had a gun in her hand.

Stupid man.

The elevator stopped with a ding, and she stepped through before the doors opened fully, almost plowing into Angie.

"Oh, hey! I was on my way to find you guys for lunch. We're ordering sushi." She rolled her eyes. "And burgers. The guys are getting burgers, Paige and I are getting sushi."

"I'll take sushi," Addison said.

"Sweet! Any preferences? We have some standard rolls we always order."

"Spicy or crunchy salmon. Or crunchy spicy salmon, if they have something like that."

"On it." She pivoted, then turned back. "You guys good? You're both…tense."

"We're fine," Addison said.

"We're good, Ange," Devon said at the same time.

She could feel the heat of his body at her back and resisted the urge to move. Mostly because she wasn't sure which direction she'd go—toward him or away from him. If she remained still, she might not have to make the decision herself.

Angie's gaze flitted between them. "O…kay. I almost forgot. Addison, Paige said to send you to her office if I found you."

"Sure. Where's her office?"

"On the far side of Graham's. I can show you." She indicated over her shoulder.

"That's okay—I can find it."

Angie nodded. "I'm going to order food. We're meeting in the conference room for a working lunch."

"You didn't ask me what I wanted," Devon said.

"Grilled chicken, whole wheat bun, spicy mayo with sweet potato fries." Angie headed down the hall. "You're predictable, Devon."

"I'm not that predictable," he grumbled. "I just know what I like."

It felt as if he'd said the last part in her ear so only she could hear it, and the vibrations from his voice raced across her skin, raising the hairs on her arms and puckering her nipples.

Away. Need to go in the opposite direction. "I'm going to Paige's office." She felt his eyes on her the entire way down the hall.

Easily finding the office, she knocked on the doorjamb and waited for Paige to finish her phone call.

She waved Addison in. "That's perfect. Can you have everything sent to Angie? ... Yes, Graham's coming. ... I suppose he's still as hot as ever, but I'm not really the person to make that judgment. ... Because that's like asking me if my brother is hot. I'm just going to tell you ew." She glanced at Addison with a questioning look.

Addison gave her a thumbs-up and nodded her head.

"Addison Foster says yes, Graham is still as hot as ever. ... Yes, she's coming as well. ... We'll discuss it this afternoon. ... Okay, see you in a few days." She hung up the receiver and swung around to pull a sheaf of papers off the printer behind her.

"What are we discussing this afternoon?" Addison asked.

"My contact is sending Angie some information on your brother and Michael Drake. We'll go over it in the conference room after we take care of this."

"Which is?"

"The contract retaining The Leonidas Corporation's services in finding and retrieving your brother. This is the same contract Michael Drake's family signed. The retainer is ten thousand dollars."

Addison's eyes widened, and she inhaled sharply. Shit. That was going to leave a mark. "Is there a cap? A point at which I can't pay anymore and you stop the mission?"

Paige rested her arms on the desk. "Addison, you don't need to sign this contract. TLC has the assets to cover the cost of the entire mission. Whether you pay or not, we're going. We don't leave our guys behind."

"You took the Drakes' retainer," she said.

"Because we didn't realize the scope of the issue when they signed it. More than likely, we'll return the full retainer."

"Then do the same with me. I'll pay the retainer, just like the Drakes did. If I get it back, I get it back. If not, it's just money." She shrugged a shoulder. Yeah, it was just money, but it was still a lot of money, and she'd feel it once her separation from the Air Force was finalized in two months.

This would wipe out a third of her savings. She should probably figure out what she wanted to be when she grew up.

"All right," Paige said.

She went through the contract, explaining the conditions and clauses. Addison initialed where indicated and signed on the last page before handing over her credit card with a hard swallow.

The paperwork finished, Paige led them to the conference room where lunch was spread out on a table at the back of the room.

Once everyone was seated with their food, Angie took a position in what Addison was beginning to think of as "Angie's spot" at the front of the room.

"Thanks to the mysterious Shady Lady, we have an invitation to the auction as well as the location." She clicked the mouse, and a picture of a fairytale castle appeared on the big screen.

"Disneyland?" Jane asked.

"No. This castle is located on the western coast of the Crimean Peninsula, inland on an estuary of the Black Sea. Using schematics I found from when the castle was put up for sale about ten years ago, I was able to render a decent three-dimensional floor plan of the building. Keep in mind, this is an estimate and not to scale, and doesn't account for any renovations made after the purchase.

"Also, can I point out there's a website to buy castles? I don't know why anything surprises me anymore, but *castles*."

"Angela," Graham said.

"Moving on. Using overhead imagery and photos of the interior that were on the website, I was able to find a smugglers' tunnel that was bricked up at some point. The team should be able to exfil that way."

"Should?" Devon asked around a mouth full of food.

"Nothing is ever guaranteed when you can't see what you're dealing with. I have no idea how thick the wall will be," Angie said.

"How big is the assault team going to be?" Addison asked.

"Not big," Paige said. "Stealth is better. We don't want to draw a lot of undue attention by blowing up a five-hundred-year-old castle."

"Our goal is to get in, free your brother and Drake, and get out without having to fight our way in or out," Graham said.

"Just the four of us inside?" she asked.

"Yes. Jane and Tinker will be outside. Turner and Harrison will be on standby for exfil," Graham said.

"But before you can get out, you'll need to take out the security system," Angie said. "According to the information I received, the security is on a stand-alone server in the castle. I can't access it remotely—it has to be taken down from the inside."

"How do we do that?" Jane asked.

"With this." Angie held up a small black circle. She pulled it apart, revealing the tiniest USB drive Addison had ever seen. "Insert this into any computer wired into the network, and then I'll be able to access the security system remotely."

"Attendees can only arrive by water," Paige said.

Addison's stomach rolled at the thought of being on a boat, and the spicy salmon rolled with it. She got violently seasick. Taking a sip of her water, she made a mental note to pick up motion sickness medicine at the pharmacy.

"We'll fly to Odessa in Ukraine. A car will meet us and take us to the port, where we'll catch a boat to the castle," Paige said. "It's a three-day party before the auction. Reportedly, there's lots of debauchery to be had. If either of you is squirmy about nakedness or sex, you need to get over it quickly."

Don't look. Don't look. She looked.

Devon's head tilted back as he chugged water, his Adam's apple working up and down as he swallowed. His other hand was clenched so hard his knuckles had turned white.

What exactly did debauchery entail?

Caught up in her musings, she didn't look away fast enough when Devon lowered the water bottle. His gaze caught hers, and the heat in his eyes scorched her. She wasn't the only one wondering what debauchery entailed.

"We'll use those three days learning the layout of the castle and grounds, filling in the gaps in Angie's rendered floorplan. We'll retrieve Braedon and Michael before the auction."

Paige's voice snapped Addison out of the sudden and sensual staredown with Devon. Braedon. Head in the game.

"The information we received indicated the women attending the auction are powerful," Angie said. "They're independent and rich, and it's not unusual for them to be serious powerbrokers within governments and international companies.

"They never attend with their husbands, even if they're married. They attend with security or lovers. That's it. You can't give the impression that Paige and Addison are in any way not what they appear to be."

"What's that?" Addison asked.

"Paige, you're going to be you—no worries there," Graham said.

Paige pointed at Graham. "You can be my security. I don't even want to pretend to kiss that hairy face."

"Addison, you're a rich, bored heiress in need of a new sex toy," Graham said.

"Don't they sell those on Amazon?" she asked. That's where she got hers, anyway.

"Yes, but not the living, breathing kind," Graham said. "Devon will be your security as well."

Graham picked up his burger and concentrated on taking a huge bite, so he missed the glare Devon shot his way.

"Addison, you and I are going shopping this afternoon. We need to get you some clothes. And a haircut," Paige said.

Angie jumped up and down, clapping her hands. "Can I come?"

"What's wrong with my clothes? Or my hair?" Addison ran a hand over the top of her head.

"If you're going to be a rich heiress, you need rich clothes and a fancy haircut. At the very least, they need to be rich-looking," Paige said.

"Why can't I be a miserly heiress?"

"We can play that off, but you're still going to need a few dresses."

"We have an early morning departure," Graham said. "Take care of what you need to take care of."

~

"Admit it, you like the dress," Paige said.

Addison turned to admire the back of the dress in the three-way mirror. Or the lack of the back of the dress. The sleeveless, deep blue shift had a boat neck and fell straight to the floor with a thigh-high slit on the side. From the front, it was demure and understated…until she turned around. Her entire back, down to the hollows in her lower back, was completely bare. If she twisted the wrong way, she felt air on the top of her butt crack.

"I like the dress."

"Good. Try on the black cocktail dress next."

Paige had told her they couldn't be seen in anything mass market, so she'd followed her to King Street and the little boutique store. They'd been there for an hour, trying on dresses, pantsuits, and various ensembles. Addison was exhausted—shopping was not her thing and she was sure the growing 'to buy' pile would cost more than she'd spent on clothes in the last five years.

She slipped out of the dress and placed it back on the hanger. "How long have you known Devon?"

"He was one of the first ones Graham hired when he started TLC, so a few years."

"What can you tell me about him?"

A beat of silence. "What do you want to know?"

"I don't know." *Everything.* "I'm going to be spending a lot of time with him the next couple of days, but he's a virtual stranger."

"You decent?" Paige asked.

Addison had just slipped her bra back on. "Yes."

The curtain opened enough for Paige to slip into the changing room with her. She turned her back to Addison. "Zip me up."

She pulled the zipper up and took the last dress off the hanger, slipping it over her head.

"He's a quiet one," Paige said. "Keeps pretty much to himself when he's not on mission. Security-wise he's clean—doesn't even speed. He likes to do everything by the book, but he'll be the first one to fire the shot if he needs to."

Paige smoothed the burgundy dress down her waist and hips, twisting to see it from different angles. "I like it. Unzip me?"

"Is there someone who's going to get upset he's going on this mission?" Addison asked, pulling the zipper down.

"As far as I know, he's not in a relationship with anyone. I don't think he's celibate, but he definitely doesn't spread the wealth like Turner. Thank God for that—I go through enough receptionists as it is."

ddison bounced her leg as the wheels of the small commuter jet returned to terra firma in Atlanta. The extra-large latte with the extra shot of espresso had been a great idea at four in the morning, but her bladder decided to wait until the last possible moment to make its needs known.

She judged the width of Devon's legs in the aisle seat. She was going to vault over him as soon as the doors opened.

"Are you nervous?" he asked.

He must have woken up when they touched down. She took in his tousled hair and sleepy eyes. That's probably what he looked like in bed. Shit. She didn't need to think about that. This trip was going to be complicated enough as it was.

"I really, really have to pee," she said.

His eyebrows rose, and then he leaned into the aisle and back. "You could probably go now."

"We're still taxiing."

"You gonna make it until we get to the gate?"

"Don't really have a choice at the moment. Just block the aisle when we get to the gate so I can run out."

He chuckled. "Will do."

After an eternity, the plane finally pulled up to the gate and the seat belt sign turned off. Devon stood and took up as much space as possible without even trying, having to duck so he didn't bean himself on the ceiling. He retrieved her small carry-on and set it in the aisle for her.

Squeezing in front of him, she bounced on her toes, waiting for the door to open. Thankfully, the three people in front of her appeared to be just as eager to get off the plane.

Devon bumped into her, throwing her off balance. His hand wrapped around her waist and splayed over her lower abdomen, pulling her flush against his front. His heat permeated through her clothes, and his fresh, woodsy scent enveloped her.

"You good?" he asked in a low voice.

No. No, she wasn't. Because now all she could think of was him wrapped around her while he bent her over something. Like a bed.

Addison swallowed twice before she could speak. "Yes."

He relaxed his arm but kept his hand high on her hip. The door opened, and she made a break for it.

"I'll meet you guys in the lounge," she said over her shoulder.

～

Bemused, Devon watched Addison do everything short of pushing the older woman in front of her out of the way before rushing off the plane. He wasn't sure how he'd ended up with the seat next to her, but he didn't really care. He'd planned to talk to her on the flight, but she'd rested her head against the window and fallen asleep. Oh, well. They'd have time on the flight to Vienna.

Graham, Paige, Jane, and Tinker were seated behind them, so Devon waited for them in the gate area.

"Where's Addison?" Graham asked.

"Nature call," Devon said. "I'll wait for her if you guys want to go ahead."

Paige checked her watch. "Make sure you're there in the next ten minutes."

"I didn't think our flight left for another three hours." Tinker pulled out his boarding pass.

"It doesn't, but we have a short window for a private conversation," Paige said. "Connie is meeting us there to give us an update."

"You mean we get to meet the Shady Lady?" Jane asked.

Paige sighed. "Do not call her that when you meet her. She will stab you."

She headed in the direction of the first-class lounge. In her blouse, slacks, and heels—with Graham beside her and Jane and Tinker following—she looked like a celebrity with her security detail. More than a few people turned to watch her as they passed.

Addison came out of the restroom, tucking her phone back in her purse. "Hey. You didn't have to wait."

"No problem. We need to get to the lounge. Paige's contact is meeting us there," he said.

Walking through the concourse, he took every opportunity to touch Addison, placing his hand on her lower back to steer her around their fellow travelers. No, she didn't need him to, but he couldn't have cared less. His palm still tingled from when he'd caught her from falling on the plane. The asshole behind him had jostled him, making him bump into Addison and sending her forward. It'd taken everything he had to ignore the small hitch in her breath when he'd pulled her against him. Remembering the throaty sound of her voice sent blood rushing to his dick.

Letting her go ahead of him into the first-class lounge, he bent at the knees and pulled at the crotch of his jeans, trying to give the family jewels a little more room to breathe.

Other than their traveling partners, no one else was in the lounge. Jane and Tinker had claimed the far corner, beers on the table next to them. Devon followed Addison to the low table Paige and Graham sat around.

A woman walked into the lounge before he could ask if Addison wanted anything to drink. A wide smile lit Paige's face when she stood and met the woman in the middle of the room, hugging her tightly. He could hear the murmur of their voices but couldn't make out the words.

They broke apart, and Paige waved Jane and Tinker over to their table. "Everyone, this is Connie Johnson. She's joining us on the trip."

That was unexpected. Devon raised his eyebrows and glanced at Graham. He didn't look surprised, so they must have discussed it earlier. He didn't know what Connie's background was, but Paige and Graham had mentioned her on more than one occasion, and she seemed to be very connected. Paige had referred to her as the Shady Lady, and that was all any of them called her from that point on.

"Connie, this is Addison, Devon, Jeremy, and Christian. And you know Graham."

"It's a pleasure to meet you." She sat in the chair next to Paige and looked meaningfully at the lounge attendant.

Devon understood when he locked the front door and left through a service door in the back.

"We have the room for thirty minutes," Connie said. She pulled small, zippered money bags from her carry-on and handed them out to everyone except Jane and Tinker.

"In those bags, you'll find passports, driver's licenses, and credit cards under a fake name. Your first names are the same, but your last names are different. I've found it's too easy to slip up when trying to remember a cover name if you've never used it.

"In Odesa, you'll give all your real personal identification—IDs, credit cards, bus pass, everything—to Jeremy and Christian. They will hold on to them for the duration."

"Why not now?" Addison asked.

"We didn't have time to book tickets in your cover name, so you have to travel on your real passports," Connie said. "Make sure you hand everything over—anything with your real name on it or anything that can be tied to who you are. My team is scrubbing any social media presence you have, which is thankfully minimal for most of you. They're also creating new profiles for you."

"You have people that can do that?" Addison asked.

"I do."

"Us, too?" Jeremy asked. "You didn't give us new identities."

"Since you aren't going to the auction, it wasn't a concern," Connie said.

Jeremy shrugged and sipped his beer. Tinker remained his usual stoic self.

"Do you know how they got my brother and his teammate?" Addison asked.

Connie inhaled and scooted to the edge of her seat. "We still aren't sure how they captured them, but they somehow ended up in the control of a member of an organization that calls themselves The Cooperative."

"Paige mentioned them before," Addison said. "Who are they?"

"They're a group of high-level crime bosses who have formed loose alliances. They cooperate when it suits them—they stay out of each other's way when it doesn't. Your brother and Michael passed through several hands until a woman who goes by the name Tsarevna got ahold of them."

"Who is she?" Devon asked.

"She's a very powerful woman in the Russian underworld. Her real name is Tatiana Olynykova. She claims to have descended from Russian royalty, so insists everyone address her as Tsarevna. In reality, she's Ukrainian. She was trafficked as a teenager and forced into prostitution until she caught the eye of a Bratva leader. He married her and, when he died of mysterious causes, she took over his role and organization. She's also part of an organization called the Council of Helen."

"Like Helen of Troy?" Addison asked.

"Yes. A strong, beautiful woman who manipulated men into fighting wars over her. The Council was originally formed to help girls who had been trafficked, to empower them and help them rebuild their lives."

"I hear a but," Jane said.

"The Council still does that, but Tatiana decided what was good for the gander was good for the goose. She traffics men and she holds these auctions three or four times a year. Invite-only and the list is exclusively powerful, sexually dominant women who participate in the D/s lifestyle."

"The what?" Tinker asked.

"Dominant submissive—BDSM," Connie said.

Tinker nodded once. His impassive face was hard to get a read on, but if he was thinking anything along the lines of Devon's thoughts, it was, "What the hell are we walking into?"

"This auction is special. She's never had American men before and for them to be military men…" Connie spread her fingers out. "I was lucky that I was able to get an invitation."

"How did you?" Addison asked.

"I've been to one of her auctions before, and we've had dealings outside of them through the Council," Connie said.

Devon had an idea she was understating her connections. Whatever organization she worked for, she was in deep.

Addison's fists clenched on the arms of the lounge chair. "If you've known about these auctions, why haven't you stopped them before now?"

"Addy," Devon said quietly, wedging his hand into her fist.

She gripped his hand tight and looked at him, tears brimming in her eyes, but he could tell they were tears of anger.

"Because until now, the men participating in these auctions have volunteered," Connie said.

"What?" Devon tore his gaze from Addison. Who the hell would volunteer to auction themselves off?

Connie moved back in her seat. "All the men volunteered as a way to work off some kind of debt—either theirs or a family member's. As reprehensible as it may be, there was nothing we could legally do about it."

"Even though they were essentially coerced into it?" he asked.

"Even though. Because we didn't have any proof. No one talked. Not the men. Not the women who won them at auction. No one." Connie looked Addison. "As much as it sucks that your brother is in this situation, it's giving us the means to take them down. As soon as we get your brother out, the castle will be raided by the authorities."

"Why not now?" Jane asked.

Connie exchanged a look with Paige and Graham. Devon could only assume they'd already had this conversation.

"Anytime the authorities have gotten close in the past, the victims were killed," Connie said. "No matter which group we went after, no matter how tight the intel, their first protocol was to kill the victims—no witnesses."

Her voice held a restrained edge of frustration and anger.

"We're not taking that chance with Braedon and Michael," Graham said. "Connie pulled some strings to let us go in first."

"Addison, your cover is you're my protégé. I'm training you to be a Domme," Connie said.

Addison blinked and opened and closed her mouth twice. "I thought I was going as a rich heiress."

"You'll be that too, but it's not enough to explain your presence at this particular auction. The only women taking part are deeply involved in the lifestyle and have been vetted by Tsarevna. This was the only way to explain why I needed an invite for you."

"What does being your protégé entail...exactly?" Addison asked.

Connie glanced from Addison to Devon and back again, her

gaze sharp and assessing. "A number of things. You may be expected to discipline Devon for a perceived infraction. You may be expected to engage in sexual activities with each other and possibly in front of others. I'll be expected to guide you and make sure you're following established rules and boundaries."

Devon didn't know which was pounding harder—the pulse in his neck or the one in his cock. When Connie said the words *discipline* and *sexual,* fuck, his mind went wild. Addison's hand had twitched in his. He was afraid to look at her, not knowing if he'd find her as curious as him…or horrified at the idea.

She looked at Addison. "You're my close friend. Shouldn't be too hard to pull off."

Paige arched an eyebrow and winked.

Connie stared at Graham. "It would be better if you were more than security."

"We've already talked about that," Paige said. "I won't be able to pull off pretending Graham and I are a couple."

"We'll figure something out," Graham said.

Connie looked skeptical, but she didn't press the issue.

"What about you?" she asked Devon. "Do you think you can give one hundred percent of your attention to Addison? Treat her like she's the only thing you care about? Do anything she asks without question?"

Addison glanced at him out of the corner of her eye, then stared down at her lap.

Not disgust, then. "I think I can pull that off."

CHAPTER 10

"*I think I can pull that off.*"

Addison couldn't get those seven little words out of her head. They repeated in her brain like a scratched vinyl record that kept skipping. It didn't help that he'd started practicing as soon as they left the lounge and headed to the gate for their flight —helping her with her bag, resting his hand on her lower back while they walked. It was disconcerting. Confusing.

Arousing.

They were seated next to each other again—this time in business class, which definitely had its perks.

"We should play twenty questions," Devon said.

"Why?"

"So we can get to know each other better. We need to know intimate details about each other. Where you're from, past lovers." His gaze dropped to her lips, and his tongue darted out. "Favorite sexual positions."

She got that *whoosh* feeling low in her abdomen that gathered between her legs. Her mouth became dry, and she fought the urge to lick her own lips or give him any indication the conversation affected her. "Why do you need to know that?"

"We're going to be in close proximity with each other. In very intimate situations. If we're going to pull this off and get your brother and all of us out safely, we have to be comfortable with each other."

It made sense. Or she wanted it to make sense, so she made it make sense.

The flight attendant announced they'd reached ten thousand feet and could move around the cabin at the same time the fasten seat belt sign turned off.

Devon unbuckled his seat belt. "We have nine hours, give or take. We have time to work on it." He got up and went to the bathroom.

Addison pinched her bottom lip between her fingers and stared in the direction Devon went until Connie surprised her by sitting in his seat.

"Hey," Addison said.

"Don't worry, I'm not staying," Connie said.

"No. I wasn't—"

"I'm teasing. How are you holding up?"

How to answer that question. "Nervous. Scared. Worried."

Connie nodded, and her light brown hair swung around her shoulders.

Her looks were remarkably nondescript. Brown hair. Blue eyes with faint lines around the corners that indicated she wasn't in her twenties, but Addison couldn't have said if she was midthirties or midforties. Average build that wasn't too voluptuous nor too athletic. Connie was pretty in an ordinary kind of way, as if she played down her looks. Which made Addison wonder again, who did Connie work for?

"How do you have all this information?" Addison asked. "Who do you work for? And why are they giving it to us?"

Connie stared vacantly for a few seconds. "I was in the Air Force for several years—that's where I met Paige. I decided the military wasn't really for me, and I ended up working for another agency."

"CIA?"

"Something like that." Her lips moved in a semblance of a smile, but it didn't reach her eyes. "When we get to the castle, you may be asked to do things that will make you uncomfortable. I will try to shield you as much as possible, but if it comes to you being uncomfortable or blowing our cover and jeopardizing this mission, I will sacrifice your comfort in a heartbeat. You and Devon need to get intimate."

Addison blinked. Had she overheard their conversation?

"Whatever arguments you're making in your head for keeping your distance? I need you to quit making them. I need you to get to that place where you can do what needs to be done without hesitation."

She held Connie's steady gaze. What places had this woman gone to? Addison nodded once.

"We'll get your brother and Michael out safely, Addison. Trust me."

She nodded again. Connie studied her for a few seconds before standing and easing into the aisle. "We'll talk more later."

Devon returned and watched Connie walk away before taking his seat. "Everything okay?"

"Yes. Just going over some things." The cabin lights dimmed, and she reclined her seat back until it was almost horizontal. Yup, business class was perky.

Devon flattened his seat and spread a blanket over his legs, kicking off his shoes once he was prone. Adjusting the pillow under his head, he sighed and closed his eyes.

Addison turned on her side, facing Devon. Although short, his eyelashes were thick, a few shades darker than his hair. He hadn't shaved in a day or two, and thick stubble covered the lower half of his face, giving him a rugged air. This close, she could see a small mole under his right eye.

Why was she fighting her attraction? Yes, the situation sucked.

Fat, hairy monkey balls sucked, but that was an excuse. A familiar excuse, if she was honest. She always found a reason not to get involved with a guy. She was deploying soon. She'd just gotten back from deployment. She was coming up on orders. Her job was crazy, and she didn't have time. If the guy was a civilian, he didn't understand the military life.

They were all excuses. She dated and hooked up, but never let it go anywhere serious. She'd watched her friends get their hearts broken and convinced herself she was better off single. But why?

Her pulse kicked up a notch, and her stomach rolled with that queasy, nervous feeling she got when she was about to step outside her comfort zone.

"Devon?" she whispered. "Are you asleep?"

"Not yet." He opened his eyes and turned his head. "What's up?"

"I've been thinking about what you said—about getting to know each other."

He rolled on his side, mirroring her position. "Okay."

"So where do you want to start?" She needed him to make the next move.

A lazy smile played on his lips. "Have you ever been married?"

She shook her head. "No. You?"

"Briefly, for about three years," he said.

"What happened?"

"I got orders to Joint Special Operations Command in North Carolina. She didn't want to leave Virginia."

Addison frowned. "Didn't she know that was a possibility?"

"Yes, but apparently she was in denial. She was not...as invested in the relationship as I was. I wanted to make it work. She wanted to stay where she was."

His voice didn't hold any hint of longing or regret. More... resignation? Chagrin?

"Nobody since then?"

Devon didn't answer right away. "Nobody serious."

His pause made her wonder. Had there been someone he wanted to be serious with?

"What about you?" he asked. "Any serious relationships?"

"Not since college," she said.

"That long?"

She shrugged. "The timing was never right."

"What happened with the guy from college?" he asked.

"He was my high school boyfriend. We dated all through college. We were supposed to join the Air Force together, but he got in a car accident six weeks before Officer Training School and had to delay. He asked me to delay as well, but I went anyway. He changed his mind and sent me a Dear Jane letter instead of coming to my graduation."

"What a dick," he said.

She smiled at his response. "Yeah. A little bit. It all worked out for the best. He found a woman that fawns all over him, and that wouldn't have been me."

"What made you decide to join the Air Force and not the Navy, like Braedon?" he asked.

"Braedon enlisted right out of high school. I considered it, but I wasn't sure if the military was the right choice for me at the time, so decided to go to college first. Once I made the decision, I didn't want there to be a chance of us being stationed together."

"Why? I thought you guys were close."

"We are, but people have a tendency to lump us together because we're twins. They assume we're the same or like the same things, even though we're completely different from each other."

"I'd say," Devon agreed. "You're much more attractive than he is."

Addison grinned. "Tell me a secret. Something no one else knows about you."

He opened his mouth and closed it as if second-guessing his answer. Finally, he said, "I follow your blog."

She cocked her head. "My blog? My deployment blog?" No one

followed her blog except Braedon, her parents, and a few of her friends.

"Yeah. Braedon shared one of your posts from your first trip to Afghanistan. The one about the coiled shit."

It took her a moment to remember. That was on her second deployment, close to ten years ago. She had a hard time recalling it, but he did?

"Oh, yeah." She chuckled. "That was gross. Thankfully, it only happened once."

His eyes flashed, and his gaze dropped to her mouth. "Your turn."

His voice was low and rough, and her body responded, sending a surge of heat to her core. She licked her lips, and he copied her, his gaze never leaving her mouth.

Time to leap. "I like to have my ass played with during sex, but I'm not big on anal."

"Fuck me." His hand shot out and grabbed the back of her neck, pulling her up and forward while he closed the distance.

She met his open mouth in the middle, her hand fisting in his shirt. His tongue thrust against hers, and she sucked it into her mouth, eliciting a deep growl. With the gentle pressure of his thumb on her jaw, he opened her mouth to deepen the kiss.

It went on and on, full of tongue and clashing teeth, sucking and biting until she was hot and achy. She wanted to be closer but the divider between their seats stopped her.

With a sharp inhale, he broke the kiss. "Scoot back."

She unclenched her fist from his shirt and shifted as far back in the seat as she could, releasing her seat belt. He stood then lay down with her in her seat.

They fit, barely, in the wide seat by lying on their sides, facing each other. The higher sides of the aisle seat provided a semblance of privacy. Yeah—business class definitely had its perks.

Devon unbuttoned her pants and pulled the zipper down slowly. "Roll over and face the other way," he said against her lips.

When she turned, he slid one arm under her neck and settled the blanket over them. Scraping his teeth against the column of her neck, he slipped his hand into the front of her pants.

"You're gonna have to stay quiet," he whispered.

"Okay." She moaned when his rough fingers teased between her folds.

"Shh." He teased the cleft, right at the top of her clit.

Easy for him to say. She pressed her ass back, and he responded by thrusting his erection against her.

He bent the arm under her neck and palmed her breast, grasping and releasing in time to the circles he rubbed around her clit.

Holy shit, she wasn't going to last long. The pressure was gentle but consistent, like a whisper she strained to hear. And exactly where she needed it, as if he had a homing beacon dialed into her pleasure.

Addison gasped as the first stirrings of her orgasm gathered. Her hand found his thigh, and she dug her fingers in and rolled her hips, riding his fingers.

"That's it, Addy," he said in her ear. "You're so hot and slick. I can't wait till I have you alone. I'm gonna bury my face right here." He swirled two fingers around her clit. "I can't wait to taste you. Fuck you. Feel you while you come all over me."

Devon thrust two fingers deep while his thumb pressed against her clit, and she detonated.

Her head fell back against his shoulder, and she pulled her lips between her teeth to keep from shouting as the spasms rolled through her.

He held her tight, slowly easing the pressure of his fingers as her orgasm subsided. "Beautiful."

"What about you?" she whispered, pressing back against him.

"Not a good idea." He straightened her pants and pulled the zipper up.

"Why not?"

"I'm a screamer."

She couldn't stop the surprised laugh that escaped.

He smiled and pressed a kiss against her neck. "Get some sleep, Addy. It's going to be a long night when we get to Odesa."

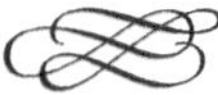

CHAPTER 11

Devon held Addison close as the golf cart wound its way up the hill. She'd started throwing up almost as soon as they'd left the dock in Odesa and hadn't stopped until a few minutes ago. Her complexion was still sallow, but she sipped on the sparkling water the porter had provided.

"You okay?" he asked.

She nodded against his shoulder but didn't open her eyes.

He stared up at the castle on top of the hill. Spotlights lit it from the base of the walls, and it loomed forebodingly over them as they approached. There was even a fucking drawbridge.

They stopped in the inner courtyard, and he wrapped an arm around Addison's waist as they passed through the huge door. It must have been a good two inches of solid wood.

The entry was opulent—gleaming hardwood floors, antique tables, gold leaf-framed beveled mirrors reflecting the light from the largest crystal chandelier he'd ever seen.

"Constance, darling! I'm so glad to see you!" An older woman entered from a room to the right, arms outstretched as she approached. Her graying hair was pulled up in a fancy hairstyle, and even Devon could tell her form-fitting dress was expensive.

"Tsarevna." Connie greeted the woman with a kiss on each cheek, European style. "I can't thank you enough for the last-minute invitation."

"It was my pleasure. Although I was under the impression you no longer attended these soirees."

"Business has kept me busy, but I still take in the occasional event. When I heard about this weekend, I canceled all my plans on the off chance you'd let me come."

Tsarevna narrowed her eyes. "How did you find out about this weekend?"

"I still talk to Alexei."

The woman's face relaxed. "Ah, dear Alexei. Is he still trying to make an honest woman of you?"

Connie's lips turned up into a mocking smile. "As if he could."

Tsarevna smirked, then looked behind Connie. "Please, introduce me to your guests."

"Of course. This is my dear friend Paige—we've known each other for ages. And this is Addison, my protégé."

"Are you all right, dear? You look a little pallid." Her lip curled up with distaste.

"A small bout of seasickness. She'll be fine after a rest."

Tsarevna didn't look impressed. "Hmm." She shifted her attention to the men. "And who are these fine specimens of manhood?"

"This is my stylist, Aiden," Paige said. "I never buy anything pretty without his approval."

Graham stepped forward, hand outstretched. Tsarevna held out her hand, and he grasped her fingers, bringing her knuckles to his lips.

"Absolutely delighted. My, you are fabulous." He turned to Paige. "If her selection is as on point as her style, we should be able to find you something absolutely exquisite."

Devon barely kept his eyebrows from going into his hairline. Graham had softened his voice and exaggerated his Southern drawl enough he could have given any blue-blooded Charleston socialite a run for her money. Guess that answered the question of how they were going to avoid having to pretend a sexual relationship.

Tsarevna bought it, placing her hand against her chest and simpering. "Oh, you are a flatterer."

"Never." Graham winked.

Devon almost threw up in his mouth, but schooled his expression when she gave him her attention.

"Mmmm. Please tell me you aren't gay. I would be very disappointed."

"No," he said.

"I'll have to carve out some time to take you to my playroom." She ran a hand over his shoulder and down his arm.

Addison growled, and he tightened his grip on her waist.

Tsarevna's eyebrow arched and she pursed her lips, glancing from Addison to Connie.

"You'll have to excuse her. He's the first toy she's had all to herself," Connie explained, "and she's still a tad possessive. I'm hoping this weekend will show her men like him can be had anywhere."

Tsarevna's shoulders relaxed and she gave Addison and Devon another appraising look. "I remember when it was all so new and shiny. Perhaps they can give us a show before the main event."

She clapped her hands together, and two men in tuxedos entered the foyer. "They will show you to your rooms. I'm sure you need to freshen up from your journey. Your luggage has already been delivered to your rooms." She gestured for their group to follow the two men.

They moved through the door on the left and up a wide, marble staircase to the second floor, their footsteps silent on the plush oriental carpet.

He and Addison were shown to a room halfway down the hall, Graham and Paige directly across from them. Connie continued farther down.

Devon guided Addison into the room and closed the door firmly, turning the ornate, old-fashioned key in the lock.

"I—"

He placed his finger over his lips, shushing her. Opening his carry-on suitcase on the end of the king-sized bed, he pulled a small hand-held AM/FM radio from the inside pocket. The clothes were rumpled enough to confirm his suspicion that their bags had been searched before being delivered, which was why they hadn't packed any high-tech equipment.

Turning the radio on, he spun the channel dial until there was no static, then walked around the room, holding it close to lamps, under tables, and near the wall sconces. It squawked on the lamps beside the bed and under the desk. He clicked it off and tossed it in his open suitcase.

Addison had remained near the door, her eyebrows pinched together and a frown on her face. Wrapping his arms around her waist, he pulled her close and slid his mouth up her neck to her ear.

"What are you doing?" she asked.

"There are listening devices in the room," he whispered. "Probably video as well. This way we can talk."

She tilted her head to the side. "Is that the only reason?"

"No. You growled." He tried to take her mouth, but she turned her head away.

"Did I?"

Was she regretting what happened on the plane? Had he misinterpreted her response to Tsarevna's suggestion?

"Yes. Push me away. Tell me to go sit in the chair, then come straddle my lap."

She shoved him away hard enough he took a step back. "Go sit in the chair."

Christ, that made him hard. He'd been suffering since the plane, and Addison standing there with her hands on her hips and an imperious look on her face about sent him over the edge.

He took off his suit jacket and tossed it on the bed, backing up until his legs hit the wide, wingback chair.

Addison didn't take her eyes off him while she sauntered to the bed and opened her overnight bag. She pulled out her toothbrush and toothpaste.

"Stay there." She shut the bathroom door, and he heard the water turn on.

He ran a hand over his mouth and grinned. She hadn't wanted to kiss him because she'd thrown up earlier. It hadn't even crossed his mind.

The water shut off, and she came out of the bathroom, kicking her heels off near the bed. She braced her hands on the arms of the chair and eased her knees on either side of his legs.

Not close enough. He grabbed her ass and pulled her tight against him, thrusting his rigid length against her.

Addison moaned and ground down on him.

He hissed out a breath. Fuck, that hurt good. "Have you ever been the aggressor?"

She shook her head.

"Now's your chance. I'm your toy—at your complete mercy. You can do anything you want to me, and I'll say thank you."

Her blue eyes darkened, and she licked her lips. "What if I want you to touch me?"

"Tell me where. Tell me how."

"On my neck—like you were before." She tilted her head, exposing the long column of her throat.

Devon nipped below her ear, then licked along her jawline. "Here?"

She moaned and rolled her hips. "Yes."

He ran a hand up the center of her back and fisted her hair at the nape, positioning her head so he could kiss her.

Her mouth opened, her tongue rubbing against his, and it was his turn to groan. Her fingers brushed against the 'V' created by the open collar of his shirt before she unbuttoned it. She spread the two sides, running her palms from his shoulders, over his pecs, down to his navel.

Fuck. He wanted her hands lower. All over his body. Clenching around his shaft as she jerked him off. He thrust up hard, and she gasped. Tugging the end of her blouse from the back of her pants, he shoved his hand in, sliding his middle finger into the cleft of her ass.

She moaned and thrust against him. Leaning back, she pulled the blouse over her head and off, tossing it aside. Her dusky-rose nipples peeked out of the lace edge of her bra.

He lifted one to his mouth, tonguing it through the thin fabric. Addison's head fell back. He pulled the fabric down and sucked her nipple into his mouth, flicking the tight bud.

"Oh!" She rocked her hips harder.

Bracing his legs, he stood and carried her to the bed, where he dropped her unceremoniously.

Her legs wrapped tight around his waist, and her fingers threaded through his hair, holding him to her breast. Like he was going to go anywhere.

He stilled when someone knocked at the door. A second knock was followed by, "Addison? It's Connie and Paige."

Her body sagged under him, and he rested his forehead between her breasts. "Fuck. Think we can ignore them?"

They knocked again. Louder. "Addison."

She sighed and wiggled under him, pulling the cup of her bra back over her boob. "I don't think so."

Devon pushed up from the bed and adjusted himself. He picked up her blouse and handed it to her. "You might want to fix your hair."

She smirked. "Why? Do I have sex hair?"

"Almost sex hair." He kissed her hard. "I'll let them in."

"Okay." She went into the bathroom, leaving the door open.

He combed his fingers through his hair, then buttoned up his shirt. Swinging the door open, he said, "Ladies."

Paige sent him an amused look. "Where's Addison?"

"Here." She came out of the bathroom, hair smoothed down and blouse in place once more.

"There's a gathering for the ladies," Connie said.

"Graham needs you across the hall," Paige said.

Devon nodded and held the door for the women, grabbing Addison's hand before she left. He kissed the back of her hand. "Be safe."

Addison glanced around the room while she sipped her wine. Every woman in the room screamed money and class. A few of them looked vaguely familiar, but without knowing who they were, she couldn't have said why. Most of them seemed to know each other and had greeted like long-lost friends. Yet they were all here to buy another human being.

She set her wine glass down on the table before she snapped the stem.

Tsarevna joined their group, sitting on the very edge of a chair and crossing her legs at the ankle. Like fucking royalty.

Maybe she should snap her wine glass. Then she could stab the bitch in the eye and be done with it.

"How are you settling in to your rooms?" she asked.

"The rooms are lovely," Connie said. "I was wondering though —are they equipped with video cameras?"

Tsarevna regarded her closely. "No. Why do you ask?"

"Oh, that's too bad. I was at a private house party a few months ago, and some of the rooms had video cameras in them, and guests could tune in to watch live. It was very…titillating." She waved a hand. "Anyway, there are a few guests I wouldn't mind peeking in on. You know I've always been more of a watcher than a performer."

"I might have to look into that for my next gathering," Tsarevna said.

"Do you have Wi-Fi anywhere in the castle?" Paige asked. "Unfortunately, I have some paperwork to complete and send back to my office, but I wasn't able to find any access points. Just once, I'd like to take a real vacation where I don't have to work while I'm away."

"I believe in keeping everyone free of distractions while they're here. But if it's pressing, I'm happy to let you use my personal office if you need to."

"I suppose I could transfer the files to a thumb drive and email them. Thank you, that would be very helpful."

A bell chimed, and Tsarevna looked over her shoulder as two large, hulking men entered the room. She stood and addressed the room. "Ladies! Your attention, please. It's time to view the merchandise."

Addison's breath sped up while her stomach cramped. The only merchandise they were there for was her brother and Michael.

One of the men went to the far corner of the room and pressed on the wall. A panel popped open, and he pulled it the rest of the way, revealing a hidden stairwell, reminding Addison of the secret doors and corridors in Versailles. The chatter in the room picked up as the women's excitement increased.

Tsarevna led them down the cool, dimly lit stone stairs. The man ducked his head and followed her.

The uneven steps wound down clockwise, and Addison heard a few of the women complain about wishing they had known they'd be exploring so they could have worn different shoes.

The stairs ended in a large chamber of stone and brick. Glancing around, she couldn't help but be impressed by the architecture. The stone ceiling was vaulted and the outline of a bricked-up archway was visible on the far wall. The flagstone floor probably wasn't original to the room.

In front of them were four doors. Large windows took up most of the wall beside each door. Tsarevna stood at the far end of the gallery, and her voice carried across the room.

"This used to be the old castle dungeon. I refurbished the space and created fantasy suites—one even still looks like an old dungeon room." Her laugh echoed off the stone walls, and Addison's hands fisted on the metal handrail.

"Is everyone here?" She craned her neck to look back toward the stairs. "Lovely. Andrew, if you would."

The man who'd opened the door turned a dial on a wall panel, and the lights lowered until it was almost completely dark. Some of the women expressed their unease until two of the windows lit up slowly, then many of them gasped.

Including Addison.

Her hand flew to her mouth. Braedon was in the room directly in front of them, sitting on a narrow bed, his back against the wall. He was shirtless, in loose lounge pants, and had lost weight. Under his short beard, his cheekbones protruded, creating hollows in his cheeks, and his muscles were less defined than the last time she'd seen him. His eyes were glassy and he stared straight ahead without focusing on anything, but he appeared to be physically uninjured—at least from what she could see. His head rolled, and he looked right at her. Tears stung her eyes and saliva filled her mouth.

She tensed to step forward, but Paige squeezed her hand—hard—bringing her back to the moment. "Keep it together," she whispered.

Addison nodded sharply and blew out a breath. He was alive. They'd work through everything else when they got him out.

Connie excused herself and moved to look in the other room, then approached Tsarevna.

"How many steps?" Paige asked in a low voice.

"What?"

"Thirty-four steps down in a clockwise spiral," she said. "How big is the room?"

Addison focused on the space. "Each room is about ten feet wide, so maybe fifty feet by thirty feet."

Paige nodded. "Do you see any variance in the walls?"

Addison realized Paige was making her think about something other than Braedon and his condition. "On the far side of the room. There's an archway that was bricked up. The bricks look old, so it was probably before this room was renovated." She should have been taking note of all this information anyway, but she was so distracted by her brother, he was all she could focus on.

Connie slipped in next to Addison and Paige. "Michael appears to be in the same condition. They're probably drugged."

"Tsarevna?" One of the women in front of them called. "Why do they look so...out of it?"

Apparently, they weren't the only ones who had noticed.

"It's a little something slipped into their water to keep them compliant. Just a low-dose sedative—nothing lasting. It's also laced with an aphrodisiac." She winked at the woman, who grinned back.

Addison tensed, and Connie slipped her arm through hers. "Easy," she murmured.

"Addison dear, you look upset. What's wrong? You don't like the idea of the men being kept docile?" Tsarevna's tone was hard, her tone provoking.

"She still has such a gentle heart," Connie said. "She'll learn."

Tsarevna stared at Addison before looking at Connie. "You always were much more patient than I was."

*D*evon used the battery lead from the radio to short out the bugs he found closest to the bed and the one in the bathroom. He knew Graham was doing the same in his and Paige's room.

A knock on the door preceded Graham slipping into the room. "Did you set up the strobe?"

"In the center window. Our room faces east, so I'm not sure how much good it will do," he said.

"Ours faces west, so Jane and Tinker should see it. We'll know for sure in the morning."

The door opened, and Addison entered, stopping just inside the room when she saw Graham. Her eyes were glassy and she was paler than when she'd gotten off the boat.

What the hell happened?

Graham reached around her and closed the door. "Are you okay, Addison?"

She jerked her head back and forth.

Devon rushed to her, taking her by the arm and drawing her into the room. "What happened? Are you hurt?"

She shook her head again, but wouldn't look at him.

"Addy, talk to me."

Instead, she eased out of his grasp and went into the bathroom, closing and locking the door behind her.

Fuck. He threaded his hands through his hair and looked at Graham.

"Get her to talk. I'll find out what happened from Paige," he said.

Devon nodded. "We'll see you in the morning."

Graham left, and Devon locked the door behind him. He sat in their chair and waited for Addison to come out. When she did, wearing a pair of sleep shorts and a T-shirt, she avoided looking at him and crawled into bed, turning away from him.

He sighed. Grabbing a pair of boxers from his suitcase, he took them into the bathroom to change. There could only be one thing to make Addison that upset—she'd either received news of Braedon or had seen him.

He wished she would trust him enough to talk to him about it. Back in the room, he draped his clothes over his suitcase and clicked off the bedside lamps before slipping into bed. The distance between them felt like miles. She was isolating herself mentally as well as physically. He couldn't let her do that if they were going to work together as a team.

Fuck, who was he kidding? Pushing him away felt personal. It was…uncomfortable having another woman withdraw from him. Except this time, he was unwilling to accept it.

"You should probably snuggle close if we're going to keep up appearances," he whispered.

"There are no cameras in the room." Her voice was rough and scratchy.

Devon rolled to the center of the bed and hooked an arm around her waist, pulling her across the bed. "Do it anyway so you can tell me what's wrong. I disabled all the listening devices, if that's what you're worried about."

She surprised him when she turned over and tucked her head under his chin. Her breath shuddered at the base of his neck, and one palm pressed against his chest while the other snaked around his back. Relief rushed through him. She wasn't pushing him away.

Wrapping his arms tightly around her, he threw a leg over her hips and enveloped her in his embrace. Her leg came up, and her thigh nestled against his cock.

He bit back the groan and kept as still as possible. She needed his comfort, not his dick.

"I saw Braedon," she finally said.

He pressed a kiss against her forehead and waited for the rest.

"That bitch is keeping him and Michael Drake drugged. He's out of it. I don't even know if he knows where he is."

"Is he injured?" he asked.

"Not that we could see. He's lost weight, though."

"What do you remember about where he's held?"

She described the room, right down to the number of steps to the dungeon, the number of lights in each room, and the bricked-up wall.

"We'll get him out. I know you're upset, but we need you to stay strong. If you need to cry or lash out, then do what you need to do. I'll be here."

"I'll be okay. I needed a few minutes to process everything by myself. I couldn't react the way I wanted to when I saw him. I needed to let it out." She inhaled deeply. "I'm scared, but mostly I'm relieved. He's alive, and now I have proof I'm not crazy."

He tightened his arms. "You growled at a woman—I don't think you should claim sanity just yet."

That got a small chuckle from her, but it was enough for now.

"Try to sleep. It's going to be a long day tomorrow."

The kiss she placed on his chest was feather-light and hit him with the force of a Mack truck.

CHAPTER 13

*A*ddison set down her empty coffee cup and leaned back in her chair. The breakfast buffet had looked delicious, but all she could stomach was coffee and toast, no matter how much Devon enticed her to eat. She just wanted to be done and gone.

Every single nerve was raw and exposed, and every laugh or smile from the other guests grated on them. She was holding on by a thread, and the unease roiling in her gut kept her tense and on edge. Not even waking up to a warm and rumpled Devon had been able to ease her tension.

A bell tinkled from the far door, drawing everyone's attention. One of the many model-gorgeous butlers, or security—whichever they were—held a crystal bell in his gloved hand.

"Tsarevna would like everyone to join her in the salon," he announced.

Devon leaned close. "Which room is the salon?"

Addison shrugged. Pushing back her chair, she joined the remaining few guests in the breakfast room as they followed the butler. They ended up in the same room they'd been in the night before. This morning, chairs formed a circle in the middle of the room.

They found Connie and Paige and joined them. "Any idea what's going on?" Addison asked.

"I have an idea," Connie said in a low voice. "Tsarevna likes public displays. I have a feeling you're about to be put on the spot."

That was the only warning they got. Tsarevna entered the room, clapping her hands.

"Take your seats, ladies. Your escorts, if they're with you, may stand behind your chairs." She strode to the center of the circle and turned slowly as if examining everyone. Stopping at Paige, she asked, "Your delightful stylist isn't with you?"

Paige laughed. "Oh, no. He doesn't wake before noon."

"Pity. I was very much looking forward to his company. Oh, well, there's always luncheon." She turned her assessing gaze to Addison before addressing the room at large. "I'd like to welcome all of you to my humble home. I always like to start the festivities off with a little guest exhibition. Normally I ask for volunteers, but I think today I'll make a special request."

She spun and zeroed in on Addison. "You and your toy can go first."

It wasn't a request so much as a demand.

"Tsarevna." Connie stood from her chair next to Addison. "Addison is still a Domme in training and has never conducted a public scene. I don't think she's ready."

"My dear Constance, what better time to learn than here with her mentor and all this experience?" She spread her hands wide, indicating the women in the circle. "You can use it as a teaching moment."

The two women stared each other down. Finally, Connie said, "I'll encourage her to do it, but I won't force her. The Council of Helen is supposed to empower women to their full potential, not take their choices away from them."

Tsarevna's gaze turned hard. She did not like being reprimanded. "Of course. No woman's choice will be taken from her here. Speak with your protégé. You should encourage her *strongly.*"

Connie pulled Addison up and led her to the far side of the room with Devon behind them.

"She suspects something, but I'm not sure what. I'll think of an excuse to give her if you can't go through with this, but it would be better if you can."

"What do I need to do? Put him in a corner while I spank him?"

"It needs to be explicit. I know it's a lot to ask, especially of two people who are virtual strangers, but if you can manage a sexual act, that will shut her up."

Addison glanced at Devon out of the corner of her eye and caught his small nod. She addressed her question to Connie, knowing she shouldn't consult with her "toy."

"I don't know what to do. I have a feeling missionary sex isn't going to satisfy her." Was she seriously considering this? More than a decade in the military had drummed "no public displays of affection" into her brain to the point she got uncomfortable with holding hands in front of people and now she had to come up with a sex act?

"It won't. The key to a D/s relationship is the exchange of control. At its most basic, a dominant controls the pleasure of the submissive. Tell Devon what to do, but don't ask. Demand it. Direct him—guide him to your pleasure, even if it's at the expense of his own." Connie looked at Devon. "If you're in any way sexually submissive, now is the time to play it up."

"I like to be restrained," he said under his breath. His eyes were downcast, his hands behind his back.

"Tied up?" Addison asked.

He nodded briefly.

A picture began to form in her head. Something she'd read in an erotic romance novel. It wouldn't be too hard to recreate, but they would both have to expose themselves—and not just physically.

"How comfortable are you being naked in front of a group of people?"

"Guess we'll find out," he said.

"Are you okay with this?" she asked.

"As long as you are."

Did they really have a choice?

"We'll do it," she told Connie. She turned and snapped her fingers over her shoulder. "Come."

She marched back to the circle and Tsarevna, smirking at her, waiting for her to refuse. Bitch had another think coming. "I need silk cord, at least three feet long. Nothing too thin."

Tsarevna gestured to one of the butlers, still staring at Addison.

"Do you mind?" Addison asked. "I don't share my toys."

Addison was an inch or two shorter than the older woman, but she still managed to look down her nose at her. Tsarevna tilted her head and walked to a seat in front of the ornate fireplace.

Going to the center of the room, she turned and regarded Devon. His full attention was on her. It was heady. Powerful. Arousing.

She'd never really taken the time to consider how alluring being in a dominant position would be. Most of the erotic romance she read involved women being dominated, not the men.

"Come here," she said. As long as she focused on Devon, she could almost convince herself they were the only ones in the room.

He stopped inches in front of her, his gaze catching hers briefly before lowering. Had he been dominated before? He seemed to know exactly what to do. A surge of jealousy rocketed through her.

"Take your clothes off. Fold them neatly and place them on my chair so they don't wrinkle."

He unbuttoned the cuffs of his shirt, then worked his way down from his collar, pulling the tails out of his pants. Shrugging out of the shirt, he shook it out and folded it lengthwise, draping it across the seat of the chair.

She really hadn't taken enough time that morning to appreciate how good he looked in a crisp white dress shirt and black trousers. Around them, the women whispered. Addison caught a few snippets—muscular, beautiful, delicious.

Devon was all those things. His muscles were defined, but she could tell he didn't skimp on his meals. A smattering of dark hair covered the center of his chest, then faded until just below his navel, where a dark trail disappeared into his pants.

He kicked off his shoes, pulling off his socks and stuffing them in the shoes before placing them under the chair. After loosening his belt, he unbuttoned his pants and pulled the zipper down. He shoved the pants over his hips, bending at the waist to pull them over his feet.

Devon went commando.

More than one woman behind him leaned over to try to have a better look. When he stood, there were several appreciative *oohs* and *aahs*. One woman even clapped softly.

He laid the pants over the shirt and glanced around. A flush bloomed over his chest.

Addison's lips twitched. He was embarrassed. A butler appeared next to her and handed her a length of black silk cord.

"Devon." She grasped his chin in her hand. "Eyes on me."

Her gaze trailed from his collarbone, down his chest and abs, and followed that happy trail farther down. His cock jumped under her scrutiny.

Damn. He was not disappointing. She'd felt it—on the plane against her ass and this morning against her thigh—but always with layers of clothes between them. Now she saw him for the first time in a room full of women. Something else to be pissed at Tsarevna about, as if she needed anything else.

"Hands behind your back, feet shoulder-width apart." She stroked her fingertips down the centerline of his torso, through the dark, springy hair around his cock.

She stroked the underside until it strained against her hand. "Good boy," she whispered.

Doubling up the length of cord, she pulled the length through the loop, creating a simple slip knot and slipped it over his cock and scrotum.

He hissed when she tightened it.

"Addison, remember to ask if he's green, yellow, or red," Connie said. "Especially when you're dealing with ligature."

She nodded and looked up at Devon. "What color are you?"

"I'm green, Mistress," he said.

His voice was strained, but his eyes were bright, almost glowing in their intensity. She felt a bead of moisture on her wrist and looked down. Pre-cum had rubbed off the head of his cock.

Addison licked the bead from her skin, savoring the salty flavor. Devon growled low in his throat, and she smirked. *Who's growling now?*

Threading the cord through his legs, she trailed a hand over his hip and the underside of his ass as she walked around him.

"Kneel," she said. She let out the cord but kept enough tension to keep it taut. She straddled his calves and wrapped her palm under his chin, tilting his head back.

"Color?" she asked.

"Green."

Maybe, but it was costing him. Sweat beaded his forehead, and his shoulder muscles twitched.

"Good boy. Arch your back."

Devon leaned back and she tied the ends of the cord to his wrists. If he pulled too hard, he'd yank on his dick and sack.

She kicked off her slingback heels next to his shoes. There was no way she was going to be able to keep her balance in those things for what she had planned next. Back in front of him, she lifted his chin to look at her. She slowly bunched up the fabric of her skirt, never breaking eye contact. If she looked anywhere else, acknowledged any of the other people in the room, she'd lose her nerve—and she needed every last bit of it to get through the next part.

This was either going to be heaven or hell for him. "Make me come."

CHAPTER 14

*H*oly shit, she was commando and his balls were on fire. She'd created a modified cock ring but gathered up his scrotum with it. Because the cord was looped, he controlled how tight it became.

Tying him up had turned her on—he could see the glisten of her arousal on the short curls around her pussy.

Leaning forward, he forgot about his hands and yanked on his nut sack. Fuck.

"Figure it out," she said. Addison wasn't going to help him one iota, and it only made him harder.

He scooted closer, putting him almost directly under her. Because of their height difference, he could sit on his haunches and eat her out. Except he kept forgetting his hands were tied behind his back and tried to reach for her. As long as he kept his hands behind him, he was fine.

He circled her slick opening with his tongue, then licked up to her clit, flicking it. He set a rhythm—circle, lick, flick. If his hands were free, he'd have grabbed her gorgeous ass and thrown one leg over his shoulder.

She tilted her hips and grabbed fistfuls of his hair, pressed against his face. She moaned and raised a leg, curling it over his shoulder. He tasted her arousal and growled his approval, pressing the flat of his tongue against her clit.

Addison shouted and thrust her pussy hard against his face, her heel digging into his back. She was faking, and he wanted it to be real.

He wanted to throw her on the floor and fuck her so hard she got rug burn on her back and left a wet spot all over the expensive Persian rug. His balls throbbed, and he felt another bead of pre-cum on the tip. His hips thrust forward, pulling the cord tight, and he grunted.

Her leg was shaking on his shoulder, the tight squeeze releasing as she relaxed. Easing up the pressure of his tongue, he lapped gently, following her lead to end things as quickly as possible.

She slid her leg off his shoulder and took an unsteady step back, pushing her skirt down. Someone handed her a napkin, and she leaned down, wiping his chin and lips. She slid her hand over his jaw and kissed him chastely before darting her tongue out to lick his bottom lip.

Her eyes were tight, but he still saw desire in them.

His own arousal coursed through him like a raging inferno. He wanted nothing more than to put her on her knees and drive his cock so deep she felt him in her throat.

Tsarevna approached, reminding him they had an audience.

"Brava," she said. "That was quite the show."

Addison blushed. She actually blushed. She'd tied him up like a steer at a rodeo and fake-came all over his face, but now she was blushing.

"Are you going to leave him like that for a while?" Tsarevna asked.

Addison's eyes flicked behind him, then back down to him.

"This was our first public performance, and he did very well. I'm going to take him to our room and let him have a reward."

"That's very generous of you." Her voice still held a hint of suspicion.

Addison stared at the older woman. "I believe in treating my toys well. Then I don't have to worry about them wandering off."

Devon knew she was playing a role, but he was getting really tired of being talked about like he wasn't there.

"Besides." Addison smiled down at him. "I have more restraints in our room."

"Then I won't keep you." Tsarevna turned her back to them. "Who's next?"

Addison leaned close to his ear. "Can you stand on your own? I don't want to untie you until we get to the room."

He nodded, not trusting himself to speak. One leg up and he realized he was going to need help. She took one of his elbows to steady him, and he managed to stand without pulling his cock off.

Hissing out a breath, he nodded, letting her know he was okay. She gathered up his clothes and their shoes and led the way out of the room. The stairs were tricky, and he had to hold his shoulders down to release some of the tension in the cord.

Addison rushed into their room and threw the clothes on the floor, shutting the door behind him.

"Untie me," he said through clenched teeth.

"I'm sorry." She fumbled with the ties at his wrists. "Hang on. Almost."

The cord whispered across the backs of his legs when it came loose. He spun and pulled her to him, slamming his mouth on hers, barely registering her moan. Lifting her, he shuffled to the bed, set her down and turned her, pushing her forward at the waist.

His dick pulsed, blood rushing through it now that the cord was loosened. Fuck, he was going to blow his load before he ever got in her hot pussy.

He pushed her skirt up, exposing her ass. Hissing out a breath, he pinched the tip of his dick, staving off the orgasm that threatened to punch him in the spine. When the worst of it receded, he rubbed the tip through her slick folds.

She moaned and tilted her hips. That was all the encouragement he needed.

He pushed forward, burying himself to the hilt in one hard thrust. He wanted to stop—to savor the moment—but she was so hot, and when she clenched around him, he broke.

He pounded into her, digging his fingers into her hips to pull her back roughly. Fuck. He wanted to make it good for her, but he was two seconds away from blowing his load so forcefully he expected his head to explode.

Slicking his thumb through her arousal, he rubbed it up and circled her anus. Her inner muscles rippled around him. He pressed his thumb in the center of her rosebud, and she clenched down on him, letting out a loud groan.

"Ah, fuck!" Thrusting twice, his own orgasm hit. He buried himself deep and shuddered.

Falling forward, he rested his head against her back. Shit. What did he just do? She still had her goddamn clothes on and he'd taken her hard.

Fuck. Fuck. Fuck.

He pulled out and stepped back, taking in the sight of her bent over the bed, her ass in the air, cum dripping down her thighs. He hadn't even thought about a condom. His cock twitched, even though he'd just come harder than he could ever remember.

Fuck!

He snatched his pants from the floor and stormed out of the room, slamming the door behind him. Shoving his legs into his pants, he yanked them up, hissing when the zipper scraped against the underside of his still semi-erect dick.

Turning toward the stairs, he realized he had nowhere to go.

He stared at the door to Graham and Paige's room, but he could not face Graham like this. Grasping the door handle to his and Addison's room, he hesitated, resting his head against the wood.

God, he was a coward. And an asshole. He knew he'd been too rough and then he'd fucked it up even more by leaving her lying there. She probably hated him now. She should. He did.

Taking a deep breath, he opened the door and slid in.

She sucker-punched him in the gut as soon as he shut it. "You bastard!"

Coughing, he bent at the waist. Holy hell, she had some power behind her. "I'm sorry. I hate myself more than you do. I shouldn't have been so rough."

"What the hell are you talking about?" she asked.

Bracing his hands on his knees, he looked up at her. "Fucking you so hard. It doesn't matter why, I should have been more gentle."

She threw her hands up. "For fuck's sake. That's why you left? You thought I didn't enjoy it? I came so hard my eyes rolled back in my head."

"It's a biological response. You didn't have a choice."

"Are you fucking kidding me?" She paced back and forth in front of him. "You really think I didn't have a choice? You think I would have laid there and let you fuck me if I didn't want you to? I was a willing participant. I wanted you to fuck me like that. One of the reasons I didn't untie you downstairs is because I knew you'd come almost as soon as the rope was loose, and I wanted to be near a bed when it happened.

"Before you so rudely stormed off to sulk and left me with your spunk dripping down my thighs, I was going to suggest we take a shower and clean each other off."

Devon pushed up to a stand. "Oh."

"Oh," she said.

He licked his lips. "Is that still an option?"

She snarled at him and stalked toward the bathroom.

He ran a hand over his face. Yeah, that was hot. If she was trying to warn him off, it wasn't working—he was stiff as steel again.

Addison didn't slam the door like he expected her to. Then the answer wasn't no? Only one way to find out.

CHAPTER 15

Addison stood under the rainfall showerhead in the middle of the huge walk-in shower that had more bells and whistles than she'd ever seen. Eyes closed, she let the hot water pour over her neck and shoulders.

Holy shit. She'd done that. She'd let someone perform oral sex on her. In public. Well…semi-public. A room full of people counted as public for her. Then she'd been fucked within an inch of her life and had come *hard*.

Her body hurt but in that good, post-sex kind of way. Every nerve ending throbbed, and she was still so unbelievably horny.

She'd been too angry with Devon leaving to tell him yes, she did in fact still want to fuck him in the shower. She might have cut off her nose to spite her face. If he didn't take the hint from the open door, she was going to punch him again, only this time much lower.

The shower door clicked open, then closed. She resisted the urge to smile. Smart man.

The flow of water stopped as he stepped behind her and traced his hands over her shoulders. "I figure you'll punch me again if you want me to leave."

She did smile then and let her head fall back against his shoulder. His muscles bunched and moved against her back.

"How does this thing work?" he asked.

A jet of water blasted her in the face. She flinched and shrieked, holding her hands in front of her to stop the spray from hitting her. Ducking to the side, she shoved her hair out of her face and wiped her eyes. So much for not getting her hair wet.

Once she was out of the line of fire, Devon took the brunt of the spray, except it hit him at the top of his chest instead of his face. He twisted knobs and pushed buttons until the spray turned off.

"That wasn't what I was going for." He wiped water off his cheeks.

Addison grinned. "That's good to know. What were you trying to do?"

"Turn off the top sprayer and turn on the lower sprayers."

"Middle knob." She pointed to the correct one.

"This one?" He turned it, and the water switched to the four jets on either side of the shower.

He scrubbed both hands over his face and slicked his hair back. "Well. So much for my artful seduction."

"Is that what you were trying to do?" she asked with a chuckle.

His gaze dropped to her breasts. Even in the steamy shower, her nipples puckered under his perusal.

He licked his lips. "Yeah."

"Wanna try again?" She stepped into the spray with him, sliding her hands from his abs, up and over his chest, to his shoulders and down his arms. Taking his hands, she placed them on her breasts.

The squeeze might have been reflex, but his thumbs circling was not. They pressed and rubbed, causing the sensitive tips to tingle and tighten even more.

"You're so beautiful," he whispered.

He cradled her jaw and dropped his mouth to hers, kissing her gently. His languid tongue rubbed against hers and the tips of his fingers skimmed down her throat and chest, around her nipples, and down. Devon ran a finger around her navel before tracing them over her hips.

His touch was so soft—barely a ghost of a whisper against her skin, like he was memorizing the shape of her body. Taking his time like he had all the time in the world. A complete contrast to earlier when he'd dug his fingers into her hips so hard.

Addison didn't know which one she preferred. Before had been hard and hot and exactly what she needed. Now, each skittering touch across her skin fueled her arousal like drops of kerosene on a low-burning fire.

She had been concentrating on what he was doing to her and forgot about what she could do to him. No audience. No one judging her performance...except Devon, and she didn't think he had any complaints.

The hair at the center of his chest was short and rough. His small brown nipples were as puckered as hers and looked like they begged to be touched. She flicked one with the tip of her tongue. Sucking on it, she scraped her teeth against it.

Devon groaned and dug his fingers into the meaty part of her ass. She grinned against his chest, kissing her way to the other nipple. He wasn't as calm as he seemed.

He palmed the back of her head. "Damn it, Addison. I'm trying to make this last."

She grasped his sack and rolled her fingers. He hissed through his teeth.

"No one's timing us, Devon. As long as we both come, I don't care how long it lasts."

He rubbed his cock between her legs. "There's no issue with me coming. It's you I'm worried about."

Addison shuddered as the tip bumped against her clit. "Do you feel that? How wet I am?"

His arm wrapped around her, and he dipped a finger into the cleft of her ass, pulling her closer.

She gasped and widened her legs.

"Yeah, I feel it," he said against her lips. He pushed her against the wall of the shower. "Guide me in."

Wrapping her fist around his shaft, she stroked from head to base a few times before guiding him where she needed him.

His other hand reached down and grabbed her leg behind her knee. "Lift your leg."

Addison wrapped her leg high around his waist as he crouched and surged up, seating himself deep in one thrust.

She inhaled sharply and dropped her head against the tile. God, he was thick. As soaked as she was, it was still a tight fit. So deliciously tight.

"Are you okay?" he asked.

He stared down at her, his face inches from hers.

"Yes."

Devon withdrew and slid forward, never breaking eye contact, and she gasped again. "You sure."

She clenched around him. "Very sure."

He groaned against her mouth and thrust into her again. His movements were measured and even, but he pressed hard each time he pushed forward.

Her hands roamed his body—over the tight globes of his ass, up his chest and shoulders. She couldn't get enough. Couldn't get close enough.

"More," she said.

"Fuck. Addy." He sped up.

Every time he hit bottom, she tilted her hips to meet him, but it still wasn't enough. That warmth in the center of her core was building but slowly. She knew if she chased it too hard, she'd lose it.

"Devon." She needed more.

"Hold on." He lifted her other leg around his hips and slammed into her.

"Yes." That was what she needed. Devon's pubic bone hit her clit each time. He adjusted his grip, and the angle of his thrusts changed so the head of his cock hit the front of her sheath.

"Oh, God. Don't stop!"

It built fast and exploded through her quicker than she expected. Not quite as hard as when he'd fucked her on the bed but surprising in its intensity. She could feel the waves rolling through as her muscles spasmed. Squeezing her eyes closed, she clenched tight around him, unable to do anything except ride it out.

"Ah, fuck!" Somehow, he laid her on the shower floor. With her legs still wrapped around his hips, he pounded into her, losing all finesse. With a shout, he thrust forward and rounded his back. His strokes shortened until he seated himself tight and shuddered.

Water swirled around them, and the only sounds were the patter of water on the tile and their heavy breathing.

Devon rested his head against hers. "We forgot the condom again."

"I'm on birth control and I'm clean." She couldn't stop touching him, running her hands up and down his back and shoulders.

"I'm clean, too." He rose up on his elbows and brushed a strand of hair away from her face. "I want to stay here—inside you, not in the shower—but we should probably check in with Paige and Graham."

That sobered her up instantly. Guilt rushed through her as fast as her orgasm had. For one blissful moment, she'd forgotten where they were and why. And yet she still wouldn't have traded that moment.

He must have read her thoughts. "Sorry I spoiled the moment."

"You didn't spoil it. Reality had to intrude at some point."

"When we get out of here, we'll find a moment with no intrusions."

CHAPTER 16

*D*evon knocked on Paige and Graham's door and glanced at Addison again while they waited. She'd been quiet the entire time they'd cleaned up and gotten dressed. Oh, she'd kissed him back when he kissed her, but he knew she was holding herself back. He just didn't know if it was because she had her head on the mission and her brother, or because she was regretting what they'd done.

The only regret he had was that it had happened under these circumstances. Any other situation, he'd still have her in bed. But they both had roles to play.

The door swung open, and Graham filled the opening. He scanned Devon up and down.

"Well, you don't look any worse for wear. I hear I missed quite the show," he said, stepping out of the way.

Devon gave a short nod and ushered Addison into the room. If that was all the grief he was going to get, he'd take it.

Connie and Paige sat on a love seat across the room. Connie gave him an appreciative once-over and raised her eyebrows suggestively. Paige refused to look at him.

"What?" he asked.

She actually held up a hand and turned her head. "I can't look at you right now. I probably won't be able to until I bleach my brain. I need to find a Man in Black to erase my memory. Preferably Chris Hemsworth."

Addison sat in one of the chairs across from the loveseat. "What's the plan for the rest of the afternoon?"

He could kiss her for getting right to the point. Actually, he could kiss her period.

"I'll ask to use the computer after lunch," Paige said. "Angie put some dummy files on the thumb drive for me to send to an email she set up. No doubt Tsarevna will check the computer to see what I did on it."

"Is she going to find the program?" Devon asked.

Graham shook his head. "According to Angie, the program will run automatically in the background as soon as the thumb drive is inserted in the computer."

"How will we know if she gained access?" Addison asked.

"Through an app on my phone," Paige said. "It looks like a game, but it's a hidden messaging program."

"Like that calculator app kids used to hide photos?" Addison asked.

"Basically, yes."

"Cool."

"Once Angie verifies she can access the security system, she'll send an update through the app," Graham said. "Christian, Jeremy, Turner, and Harrison will get the same update. We'll be able to coordinate the extraction with everyone. They're on standby so, if all goes well, we'll get Braedon and Michael out tonight."

Addison leaned forward and rested her head in her hands.

Devon sat on the arm of the chair and rubbed her back. "What's the plan for the rest of us while Paige is sending emails?"

"We're going to scope out the perimeter of the castle—as much as we can," Graham said. "If we can find the entrance to the tunnel, we'll mark it to make it easier for Tinker and Jane to find."

"What about after?" Addison asked. "How are we getting out of here?"

"All we have now are the basics," Graham said in a low voice. "Get Braedon and Michael out. Exfil through the tunnel, if possible. Boat back to Odesa, plane to Germany."

"That sounds like a gross oversimplification of the mission," Addison said.

"It is," Paige said. "Right now, there are a lot of unknowns. I haven't seen any armed security, but that doesn't mean Tsarevna's 'staff' aren't carrying. I've seen a few cameras, but there could be many more that we don't know about. We don't know if there is security on the perimeter."

"So, we're going to wing it. You can say we're winging it," Addison said.

"Not if we can help it. That's why Paige needs to get access to the computer and why we need to do recon this afternoon," Devon added.

Her back rose and fell under his palm, and she nodded shortly.

"Improvise, adapt, overcome," Graham said. "We've done more with less information. We'll get everyone out of here in one piece."

Connie checked her watch. "We should go down to lunch. Dinner tonight is going to be formal. If she follows her usual schedule of events, there will be a floor show after dinner. Attendance is expected—participation is optional but again, highly encouraged."

"Oh, joy," Addison said.

"I think you'll be exempt this go 'round," Connie said.

"Thank God." Paige dramatically threw herself over the arm of the sofa. "No offense, Addison, but I don't want to see any more naked Devon. There are just things I shouldn't know about co-workers."

"You're never going to let this go, are you?" Devon asked.

Paige stood and smoothed down her skirt. "Nope. I've already shared it in the group chat. Just be glad I was too traumatized to take pictures."

Graham slapped him on the shoulder. "Don't worry, I drew one."

"You weren't even there."

"I used my imagination. Sorry, Addison, I took artistic license and replaced you with a sumo wrestler."

That coaxed a small smile from her. "Woe is me. I don't think I'll ever recover from the slight."

"I'll see what I can do next time," Graham said.

"No," Devon said. "No next time. No more pictures. No more public nakedness."

"Okay." Graham smirked.

"Tsarevna seemed pretty disappointed you weren't there. Maybe she'll make you get naked. Then I can draw pictures."

"Bring it on, Picasso."

"Children!" Paige glared at them from the door to the room, one hand on her hip and the other on the handle. "Don't make me separate you."

He and Graham looked at Paige and then each other. "Yes, mother," they said in unison.

Paige stared up at the ceiling. "I don't get paid enough for this."

She flung the door open and stormed through.

"Just make sure you get my proportions right," Graham said, walking out after Paige.

"I need a can of Vienna sausage for comparison!" Devon called after him.

"Wait." Connie stopped them from following Paige and Graham. "Devon, at lunch and dinner, you need to walk two to three paces behind Addison. Hands behind your back, eyes down. Lunch is informal, but you need to seat her at the table and then wait for her to tell you to sit."

"Really?" Addison asked. "He's not a dog."

"No, he's not. What he's supposed to be is a submissive, and there may be subs sitting at their Dommes' feet like dogs. I realize this is a crash course in a lifestyle you're not in any way familiar with, but trust me. This is the basic behavior expected of a submissive at this party."

Addison bit the corner of her lip and looked up at him. Devon shrugged. As long as he wasn't trussed up like a Thanksgiving turkey and put on display in the center of the table, he didn't really care.

"What about while we're walking around outside?" he asked.

"Act how you normally would, but inside the castle—especially around other people—you need to play your roles."

"How am I supposed to address him?" Addison asked. "Or him me?"

"He should call you Mistress, like he did earlier. You can address him however you like." Connie glanced between the two of them. "You both did really well earlier. I know Paige and Graham are giving you crap, but for newbies and virtual strangers, that scene was really well done. Neither of you have any experience in the life?"

"Outside of reading erotic romance, no," Addison said.

"My porn collection is fairly standard," Devon said.

"Well, keep doing what you're doing," Connie told them.

They stared after her for several moments. The silence was bordering on uncomfortable.

Before he could ask if she was ready to go to lunch, Addison whispered, "I don't know if I can keep doing this. Are you okay with this?"

He brushed the backs of his fingers along her chin. "You've got this. Just imagine you're ordering around brand new butter bars fresh out of OCS."

That got him a quick smile. "I'm sorry ahead of time," she said.

"For what?"

"Because when we walk out of this room, I'm going to be the bitchiest bitch that ever bitched."

He grinned. "Lead the way."

Addison took a deep breath and marched out the door. Devon pulled it shut behind him and fell in behind her, arms behind his back, eyes on the backs of her shoes. The off-white pants she'd changed into hugged her hips and ass. He didn't mind having to trail behind her at all.

They entered the dining room—more formal than the room where they'd had breakfast. Addison paused just inside the entrance. Taking a chance, he glanced up and scanned the room. A table stretched almost the entire length of the room and damned if there wasn't a man wearing a collar and leash around his neck sitting on the floor next to a woman.

Devon's butt cheeks clenched when he saw the man had a tail. Considering he was naked except for the collar, it didn't look like a clip-on. Other men stood behind chairs, some knelt next to them, one woman sat on the lap of one man while another fed her.

In the pale blue button-down shirt and black slacks, Devon felt overdressed compared to the other men in the room since the vast majority of them wore little to no clothing.

Addison stopped behind a chair next to Paige. He pulled it out and then helped her scoot in. And waited.

Several moments later, she snapped her fingers and shook her head. "Hello? Food?"

Devon startled, but recovered quickly. "Yes, Mistress."

"Get plates for Paige and Connie as well," she said.

He nodded and went to the food-laden tables set up along the side of the room. Under normal circumstances, he'd ask what she wanted but since he should know what she liked, being her toy and all, he selected food he thought she'd want based on the few meals they'd had together. He fixed additional plates for Connie and Paige and carried them back to the table, setting them in front of the ladies.

"Where's mine?" Graham asked with a shit-eating grin.

Devon's mouth pinched, and he glared at his boss.

"You can get your own," Addison said. "Devon needs to feed me before he eats. Sit." She pointed at the chair next to her.

Devon smirked at Graham before pulling out the chair next to Addison. He spread a cloth napkin on her lap and cut a small piece of prime rib to feed her.

Watching the fork slide sensuously from between her lips had his cock tenting his pants within seconds. He would never describe himself as submissive, but he understood the appeal of this lifestyle. Maybe not the dog tail butt plug part, but serving someone, seeing to their needs, making them happy…that he got. Aside from walking behind Addison and assuming a submissive pose, he wasn't doing anything he wouldn't do if they were in a real relationship.

If they were in an actual relationship, he'd go to the ends of the earth to make her happy.

"Tsarevna?" Paige stopped the woman as she passed. "Would it be possible to use your computer after lunch? I'd like to finish my work so I can enjoy the rest of the afternoon."

"Of course," she said. "I'll have one of my staff escort you. Is thirty minutes enough time to finish your lunch?"

"Plenty of time, thank you."

"Tsarevna, is there a path down to the water? Other than the one we came up on from the dock?" Addison asked.

"I believe so, why?"

"I've never been to the Black Sea. I like to take pictures of my feet in different bodies of water. Proof that I've been there."

He didn't know if that was true or not, but it presented the perfect cover for asking.

A patronizing smile formed. "How quaint. Yes, there are

several paths that lead down to the water. Any of the staff can direct you."

Addison returned Tsarevna's fake smile with one of her own. "Thank you."

She took the fork from Devon's hand. "Go eat. I don't want to be stuck inside all afternoon."

"Yes, Mistress," he said in a low voice.

CHAPTER 17

*A*ddison stopped halfway down the well-worn yet steep path and stared back up at the castle looming behind them. The wind gusted, whipping her hair around her face.

"Everything okay?" Devon asked.

She nodded. "Yeah, just getting my bearings."

They continued down to the crescent-shaped beach. Checking her watch, she noted it had taken them about fifteen minutes to walk down from the castle, but they hadn't been in a rush. Cliffs enclosed the beach, protecting it from the worst of the wind.

"I think the cave entrance is that way," Connie said, pointing to the taller cliff at the north end of the beach.

"Why?" Addison asked.

"Because that's where the butler said it would be."

"He didn't find it suspicious that you asked?" Devon asked.

"I didn't ask. He said if I was interested in playing pirate, there was a cave in the north cliff that guests liked to use. Apparently Tsarevna held a themed party last year. Two guesses what the game for that party was." She winked at Addison.

"Find the booty?" Graham asked.

"Followed by a rousing game of bury the treasure," Connie said.

"At least she's inventive," Devon said.

They heard voices and glanced up the path. Two women made their way down, trailed by two men. The women waved when they saw them.

Addison and Connie waved back.

"Should we still check out the cave or should we wait?" Addison asked.

"Let's get a little more cover," Graham said. When the group reached the beach, he raised an arm. "Argh! Have ye come to follow me treasure trail?"

"What treasure trail?" the woman with brown hair asked.

"The one that goes down here." His hands moved to the button of his pants, as if he was going to take them off.

Connie smacked him on the chest with the back of her hand. "Stop. Don't mind him. We were told there was a cave in the cliff, and he won't stop making innuendos about booty and treasure trails."

"How exciting!" the other woman said. "I want to see it." She turned to the man closest to her. "Hector, carry me. I don't want to get sand in my shoes."

"Yes, Mistress." Hector picked her up and cradled her in his arms. With his dark hair and complexion and her platinum blonde hair, they looked like a couple on one of the bodice ripper romances Addison's mom used to hide in her closet.

"Lead the way!" the woman said.

"Yo! Ho ho!" Graham raised his arm like he held a sword and started down the beach, his new entourage in tow.

"Is he always like this?" Addison asked Devon. She would not have expected this role from him based on their interactions back in South Carolina.

"Sometimes, yeah. Graham knows how to relax and have fun,

but when it's go time, it's go time. He's one of the few officers I'd willingly follow into combat."

They trailed behind the group, and Addison stopped every now and then to pick up a shell.

"What are your plans after we get home?" Devon asked.

"I don't know," she said. "I haven't given much thought beyond finding Braedon."

"What do you want to do?" he asked.

She shrugged. "No idea. I always figured I'd retire from the Air Force and I'd have plenty of time to figure out what I wanted to do afterward. I guess I could go back to school and get my PhD."

"You don't sound too excited about that." He bent down and scooped up a flat pale rock.

"Yeah." She had no desire to go back to school, but if she wanted to use her degree in psychology, she'd have to.

"What are you passionate about? What excites you?"

You.

But she couldn't say that. They weren't there. Yeah, they'd had some seriously awesome sex, but sex didn't mean feelings, and past experience had taught her not to equate orgasmic endorphins with feelings of the heart. Most guys cut and run at the first hint of a lasting attachment. Easier to stay detached. That way she could shrug and move on when he did.

Plus, she needed to take Braedon home. Her parents…God, how was she going to handle that? How were they?

"Addison?"

Right. Passion. Excitement. "Honestly? I don't know anymore."

Devon threw a rock, skipping over the gentle surf. "What if you—"

"Hey! We found it!"

They looked down the beach. Connie waved her arm for them to join them.

"What if I what?" she asked.

He shook his head. "Later. Let's find out what's in the cave."

She thought about telling him no and forcing him to finish his question, but the rest of the group was waiting for them at a rocky outcropping at the base of the cave.

The entrance was about five feet up, and they had to climb up the rocks to reach it.

"Did anyone bring a flashlight?" the blonde woman asked.

Devon pulled his cell phone from his back pocket and turned on the light.

"Oh." The woman stared at the phone a moment and then laughed. "I swear I'm not really this airheaded."

"It's okay," Addison said. "It didn't occur to me either."

With five lights shining, they could see fairly far into the cave.

"Where do you think it goes?" This question from the brunette.

"Let's see." Connie set off, shining the light from her phone ahead of her.

More of a tunnel than a cave, three of them were able to walk side-by-side without touching the sides. The women were able to walk without stooping, although Devon, Graham, and one of the other men had to dip their heads in a few spots to avoid hitting the ceiling.

"Do you think there are bats?" the woman closest to Addison whispered.

"Probably," Devon said, directing his light overhead.

Nothing moved on the ceiling that they could see, but that didn't stop the woman from grabbing onto Addison's arm.

"They're more afraid of you than you are of them," Addison said.

"That's what they always say," the woman said. "Until they get attacked by a rabid vampire bat."

"Pretty sure vampire bats aren't found in Europe," Addison said.

"How sure?"

"Ninety-nine point nine percent."

"Okay. But I'm still going to walk next to you—you're taller, so they'll get caught in your hair first."

Addison chuckled until she remembered the woman was there to try to buy her brother. Why did she have to be so normal?

They walked on in silence until they reached a brick wall.

"Huh," Graham said. "I wonder if this went up to the castle at some point."

Addison frowned. He already knew the answer—it was why they were there in the first place. She glanced at Devon, and he tilted his head at the woman next to him. Ah. Graham was asking for their benefit.

"Why on earth would they need a tunnel to go up to the castle?" the blonde asked.

"Smugglers, probably," Graham said. "This would have been the perfect place to smuggle contraband during the Cold War. And there really were pirates that roamed the Black Sea a few hundred years ago."

"Well, this is anticlimactic," the brunette said. "Let's go back to the castle. I want a real climax." She snapped her fingers, and the other man fell in behind her.

The blonde sighed. "Well, thanks for letting us tag along. Come on, Hector."

The entrance wasn't visible from the end of the tunnel since it had curved into the cliff face. They waited until the women's voices were nothing more than a whisper.

"Shine your flashlights on the wall so I can get a couple of pictures," Graham said. "Devon, what was your distance?"

Addison's eyes widened. Were they supposed to have measured the distance?

"Two hundred meters. Maybe two-fifty. My steps were shorter, so it was hard to judge."

"I got the same," Graham said. "Addison, how tall are you?"

"Five-six. And a quarter."

"Stand in front of the wall with your arms stretched out."

She did as he asked, holding her arms as straight as possible until he nodded at her that he had what he needed.

"I can't get a location on my phone," Devon said.

"We'll get a reading at the entrance. I'll get one from inside the castle as well. That'll give us an approximate distance from the cells." Graham scratched at the mortar around one of the bricks. "It's crumbling."

He pulled a multi-tool from his belt and flipped it open. Scratching at the mortar around a brick, he scraped enough away that he was able to push the brick through to the other side. He shined his light into the small opening.

"It looks like it goes another twenty or thirty meters, then there's another wall. It's arched, from what I can tell."

"That's probably the portion we saw in the dungeon," Addison said.

"Can we push this one down now?" Connie asked. "Save time later?"

"Better not," Devon said. "Other groups may come in here to check it out. If we knock down the wall now, it would get back to Tsarevna."

"What about the brick Graham knocked out?" Addison asked.

"I don't think anyone will make a big deal over one brick, but it does make things easier for us. One less explosion."

"Let's head back out," Graham said. "That other group might get suspicious if we stay in here too long."

Addison's feet felt rooted to the spot. She didn't want to leave. Braedon was only yards away—they were so close.

Graham grabbed her shoulders. "Hey. Twelve hours from now, we'll have him. We have what we need to make that happen, but we need to be smart about it."

She swallowed hard and nodded. He was right, but that didn't mean she had to like it.

"All right. Let's go," she said.

He led the way out of the tunnel. Just shy of the entrance, he stopped and dug something out of his pocket. It looked like a clear Lego with electronics inside.

"Firefly beacon?" she asked.

"Yes. Here." He pulled out another beacon and nine-volt battery from his pocket. "We need to set these up on either side of the tunnel. High enough that someone won't be able to see them unless they're looking for them, but so that they're still visible from the outside."

Addison snapped the small infrared strobe to the battery. The rock jutted out in places, and they found sections large enough to set the strobes on so nothing blocked them. Even with something in front of it, the infrared strobe would be visible with night vision goggles, but invisible to the naked eye.

The two couples were still on the beach when they exited, but farther down. Addison sat on the rocks below the entrance and took off her shoes.

"What are you doing?" Devon asked.

"Taking a picture of my feet in the Black Sea." She rolled her pants legs up to her knees and stepped into the water, gasping when the tiny waves lapped at her ankles.

"Cold?"

"Little bit." She aimed her phone down and snapped the picture.

"Do you really do this or did you just come up with it today?"

She stepped out of the water, back onto the rocks, and used the cuff of her light sweater to dry her feet.

"I really do this."

Shoes back on, she leaped off the rock onto the sand, turning to look back at the cave one last time. They found it. She closed her eyes and sent out a silent plea. *Please let this work and everyone get out of here safely.*

CHAPTER 18

They followed Graham to his and Paige's room. Not for the first time, Devon wondered how that worked since there was only one bed. Not that he wondered hard. He had no more interest in his bosses' sex lives than they had in his.

Paige was curled up in one of the chairs, typing on her phone. "Hey. How was the beach?"

Graham sat in the chair perpendicular to hers. "It was a beach. It's not the Keys, but then nothing is. We did find an old smugglers' tunnel. That was interesting. Were you able to finish your work?"

"Yes, thankfully. I also talked one of the butlers into giving me a tour of the castle." She touched her phone screen and handed it to Graham. "Now I can enjoy the rest of the weekend without interruption."

"Wonderful. Stress isn't good for your complexion. It makes you sallow, and my job of making you look fabulous that much more difficult. I can only work with what I'm given after all."

Graham smirked when Paige flipped him off.

"Did you get the delivery I arranged?" Connie asked.

Paige nodded. "I did. How did you manage that, exactly?"

"I have someone in the castle," she said.

"Wait," Addison said. "You have someone here? Right now?"

"Yes."

"Who? Are they going to help us tonight?"

Connie shook her head. "Better that you don't know. If everything goes well, he'll stay here to facilitate the raid after we leave."

"Makes sense," Graham said as he passed Paige's phone to Devon.

"What gear?" Devon asked, taking the phone.

"Some protective gear and firepower," Connie said. "You have the same items in your room."

Devon nodded and focused on the screen in his palm. Angie's app was open to the messages. She'd accessed the security system and would take everything down at zero three thirty. As a bonus, she'd completed the layout of the entire castle and figured out a way to take all the power out to make it look like a malfunction in the electrical system.

The weight of Addison's breasts pressed against his arm, causing his dick to stir. Jesus. He'd never had a problem controlling his reaction around a woman, but he constantly had at least a semi, if not a full-on raging erection, whenever she was near.

"Does the information get updated in the app, or is it sent to one person specifically?" Devon asked.

"The app updates," Paige said.

"So we all have the information?"

"Yes."

Addison pressed her head against his upper arm, and her breath feathered against the skin below the edge of his shirt sleeve.

"Are you okay?" he asked.

She nodded. "A little tired. I think I'll take a nap before dinner."

"A nap does sound good right now," Paige said.

"You haven't done anything all day," Graham said.

Paige shoved his leg with her bare toes. "My brain worked hard today."

"Oh, well, in that case, I can understand why you're so tired."

"Whatever. We'll meet around seven forty-five for dinner," Paige said.

"See you then," Addison said.

Devon handed the phone back to Graham. "Let us know if anything changes."

Addison headed to the bathroom as soon as they got to their room while Devon went to the large duffle bag on the couch. Unzipping it, he found two backpacks, his and Addison's vests, communication devices, holsters, weapons, ammo, and two sets of night-vision goggles. Damn. Connie had really come through. One of these days, he'd figure out who she really was and how she was connected. Today, he was simply glad she was on their side.

He kicked off his shoes and stretched out on the bed, arms stacked behind his head. When Addison returned to the bedroom, she lay down next to him, not touching.

"Will you go back to Texas when we're done?" he asked.

"I suppose. My parents will probably want Braedon to stay with them once the military's finished reintegrating him. At least for a little while."

"And you'll want to be close to Braedon." It made sense that she'd want to be near her family. "Will you stay in Texas?"

"No." She rolled on her side, facing him, and tucked her head into the pillow. "Was that what you were going to ask me?"

"When?" he asked.

"On the beach. You started to ask me something but got interrupted," she said.

Now was his chance. A small window of opportunity to ask her to come to Charleston after Braedon was rescued and settled. And he didn't have the balls to do it. Not tonight. She was worried about the extraction. He didn't blame her—he was nervous as well, but not any more than usual before an op. There were a lot of moving parts and unknowns, and so many things could go wrong.

Which is why she needed to be focused on the mission. Not his need to figure out what happened next.

He shook his head. "Something like that. I don't remember exactly."

Her blue eyes searched his for several moments. "Maybe you'll remember later."

"Maybe."

Her eyelids lowered but didn't close all the way.

"What's going on in your head?" he asked.

"I'm scared," she whispered. "If something goes wrong..."

"Hey. Come here." He gathered her in his arms, tucking her close to his side so her head rested in the pocket of his shoulder. "I'm not going to promise everything's going to go according to plan—no plan survives first contact with the enemy. But we know what we're doing, and we will get Braedon and Michael free."

He angled his head back to look at her. "Believe me?"

She nodded against his chest.

"Good. Try to get some sleep. It's going to be a long night."

When he woke a few hours later, the spot next to him was empty and the shower was running. Briefly, he considered joining her. He checked his watch, noting they had a little more than an hour before they had to meet for dinner. That might give him enough time to get ready afterward, but it probably wasn't enough for Addison.

But imagining her in the shower, running her soapy hands over her tits then down her stomach to her sweet pussy, only fired up his libido. Palming his dick through his jeans, he rubbed the rough fabric over the sensitive skin. He needed to rub one out before dinner and he didn't want to wait until he was in the shower.

Unfastening his pants, he wrapped his hand around the shaft while picturing Addison. Was she as horny as he was? Was she getting herself off in the shower? Did she use her fingers or one of the detachable shower heads?

The image morphed so he was in the shower with her, using the shower head along with his tongue. A bead of pre-cum escaped, and he squeezed his eyes closed, pressing his head into the pillow.

Something warm and wet licked the tip of his dick, and he jerked.

"What the hell?"

Addison stood next to the bed, wearing a towel and a smirk and nothing else.

"Jesus. Addison, you scared the crap out of me." He'd been so caught up he hadn't noticed the shower turn off.

"I see that."

He moved to tuck himself back into his pants—he'd finish in the shower.

"Ah ah." She pushed his hands aside and wrapped hers around his cock.

Devon hissed through clenched teeth. The mattress dipped next to his hip as she climbed on the bed, settling between his legs. He spread them farther apart to give her room.

"Addison—"

"Someone's been naughty and needs to be punished." She licked the very tip of his head.

"Shit. I don't think you understand the definition of punishment," he said.

"Hands under your head. Keep them there or I stop."

He followed her instructions, shoving his hands under the pillow and fisting the fabric in his hands.

"Good boy." She licked around the head of his dick before slowly sliding her mouth down the length.

He spread his knees wider when she drew her mouth up the shaft, the tip of her tongue pressing against the underside.

"Fuuuuck," he groaned.

Grasping the base of his cock with one hand, she set a slow, steady rhythm with her mouth and fist. Up and down, twisting her fist.

Maybe she did understand the definition of punishment because he teetered on the precipice of an orgasm forever. She didn't change her pace, and it hovered just out of reach. Every time he tried to thrust his hips up or speed up, she backed off. His whole body shook, every muscle straining with the effort to be still and accept what she was giving.

"Addy, baby." He wasn't even sure what he was asking for.

She shifted and grasped his ball sack in her other hand, rolling and squeezing in time to her mouth. There it was. It started to gather in the base of his spine, and his balls drew up even as she pulled on them.

One of her fingers rubbed his perineum and, holy fuck, she slid the finger forward, farther into his ass and pressed against the entrance at the same time she took his cock deep in her mouth and swallowed.

"Fuck me!" His orgasm exploded out of him, and his back bowed off the bed. His hips thrust mindlessly as he spurted his seed. Shit. Every time with Addison was better than the last.

She released him with a soft lick and swirl of her tongue and crawled up his body to lie on top of him, her head in the crook of his neck.

It took every last bit of his strength to wrap his arms around her, one hand on her ass. He blinked his eyes open. "Jesus. Are we going to be late for dinner?"

"No. We've got about forty minutes. I didn't wash my hair so I just need to do my makeup while you take a shower."

"It's only been twenty minutes?" he asked.

"Eh. Closer to fifteen."

"I don't know what to say. Thank you. I'd like to return the favor, but I'm finding it hard to move."

She laughed softly. "That's okay. I took care of myself in the shower."

He squeezed her ass. "Fuck. That's what I imagined. That's why I started stroking one out."

She propped herself up on his chest. "Why didn't you join me?"

A thick strand of hair had escaped her bun, and he tucked it behind her ear. "I didn't want to make us late."

She grinned but her smile faded. "Are you okay with all this?"

"All what? The awesome sex?"

That got a little of her smile back. "The power dynamic we have to present outside this room with you acting like my submissive. I'm having a hard time staying in character. I don't want a pet or a toy. You don't find it...degrading?"

"I've got a buddy down in Tampa who owns a BDSM club. I've visited a couple of times, but never took part in anything."

"Why?"

"I wasn't dating anyone and I didn't want to take part in a scene with someone I didn't know."

"You didn't know me," she said.

"I did, kind of. Through Braedon." It was a chickenshit answer. He should have told her he'd known her for a long time, even if it was from afar. "But back to your question about whether I find this degrading. I don't. I know some people, men and women, get off being degraded. For some, it's a power exchange. For others, it's sexual gratification. In every situation I've ever seen, the dynamic between a Dom and sub is one of trust and respect between consenting adults...even when it involves wearing a dog tail butt plug and eating out of a dog bowl."

Addison rested her chin on her hands. "These women are here to buy my brother and Michael."

"Yeah."

"There's nothing consenting about that," she said.

"No, there's not."

She closed her eyes and a tear rolled down one cheek. "I want to burn this place to the ground with every one of them in it."

"Let's concentrate on getting your brother and Michael out first, then we can explore mass murder options."

She nodded and blew out a breath. Rolling to the side, she slid off the bed. The towel fell to the floor, exposing the sensual curve of her back as she walked over to her suitcase.

"Better hop in the shower or we will be late," she said.

Devon ran a hand over his mouth. It might be worth it.

CHAPTER 19

*D*inner was a formal, lavish affair. Soft candlelight filled the room as course after course was served to them by men wearing nothing but stiff white tuxedo collars and cuffs. None of the other guests blinked twice at having a penis hovering next to them while being served a dish, but Addison pushed her food around the plate looking for any stray hairs before eating.

When the first course was removed, Graham leaned over and whispered, "I hope spotted dick isn't on the menu."

He said that right as she had taken a sip of wine that went straight up her nose. It was that or spew it at Connie, sitting across the table from her.

Devon handed her a napkin from his position behind her chair. Some of the submissives knelt at their Dommes' sides, while others stood behind the chairs like Devon did. They ate standing up. Addison didn't like it, but the seating had been assigned, and there were no seats available for any of the subs. Graham was the only man seated at the long table since he was Paige's "stylist."

The conversation wasn't any different than the few dinner parties Addison had attended. They discussed politics, world events, and Paige and the woman beside her got into a heated debate about college football teams.

It was all so normal. As long as she ignored the woman next to her getting eaten out. Addison vacillated between turned on and awkwardly mortified.

Devon leaned close and whispered, "Are you going to ask for what she's having?"

She had to press her lips together to keep from laughing and she shooed Devon away from her ear.

"Tsarevna," a woman called from the far end of the table. "I have a question about tomorrow's activities."

The level of the conversation lowered as everyone turned their attention to their hostess.

"Of course, Lydia. What would you like to know?"

"How did you obtain the merchandise?"

Addison clenched her fist around the knife in her hand so hard one of her knuckles cracked. Graham rested his hand on hers and pushed it against the table until she released the knife, then held her hand in his.

Tsarevna sipped her wine. "I don't see why it's important, but if you must know, they came to me through a middleman."

"But they're here willingly?" Lydia asked.

"Well, they haven't voiced any objections." Tsarevna offered that patronizing smile of hers.

Addison wanted nothing more than to punch that stupid woman in the face.

"Are they capable of voicing an objection should they have any?" Lydia asked.

Maybe not all the women here were as blasé about auctioning off unwilling human beings as they appeared.

Tsarevna remained silent, lifting her chin a fraction and staring down her nose.

Lydia set down her silverware and wiped her mouth with her napkin. Setting the napkin next to her plate, she stood. "I'm afraid something has come up. A pressing matter I must see to immediately and I'll need to leave tonight. I would appreciate if you arranged for the boat to take me to Odesa in an hour."

Tsarevna's lips pinched at the corners. "Has anyone else had a pressing matter arise that requires them to leave immediately?"

Three other women stood from the table.

"How unfortunate." She raised a hand and beckoned to one of the men behind her. "Have the boat here in an hour to take these guests back to Odesa."

She turned her attention back to Lydia and the other women. "You understand if you leave tonight you will not receive any future invitations."

"Completely," Lydia said. "You've strayed too far from the vision of the Council, Tatiana. I want no part of it." She left the dining room, the man with her trailing behind. The other women left as well.

Addison stared wide-eyed at Connie. *What just happened?* she mouthed.

Later, Connie mouthed back.

Graham leaned close. "I think we just witnessed a coup," he whispered.

The tension and anger emanating from Tsarevna were palpable. Conversation was slow to start back up, everyone speaking in hushed tones and whispers. Halfway through the fish course, cutlery clattered against a china plate, startling more than one person.

Tsarevna pushed back from the table and left the room.

Everyone glanced around at each other, wondering what they should do.

A butler entered through the doorway she had stormed through. "Tsarevna is not feeling well and has retired for the night. Tonight's exhibition has been canceled. Tsarevna bids you all a good evening. Dinner will continue." He bowed, executed an about-face, and left the dining room.

A brief moment of silence was quickly overtaken as conversation erupted around the table. Addison caught snippets.

"I've never seen her this angry."

"She and Lydia have known each other for years."

"Do you think the auction will still go on tomorrow?"

The last question had her clenching her fists again.

"Easy," Graham said. "This will likely work to our benefit."

Inherently, Addison understood any kink in Tsarevna's normal routine and plan worked to their benefit, but she struggled to sit there with a fake smile on her face while these women discussed purchasing two people. Never mind one of them was her brother, they were people! Human beings with lives and families who missed them.

"Well, that was an interesting turn of events," the woman next to her said.

"Why do you say that?" Addison asked.

"Lydia is—was—Tsarevna's staunchest supporter. She was one of the first members of the Council of Helen, but as she gained more public prominence, her role in the Council became quieter."

"Who is she?"

The woman smiled. "You don't recognize her?"

Addison shook her head. "No, but I don't really pay all that much attention to celebrity gossip."

"I suppose it makes sense—Americans never pay any attention to the monarchies unless they're British. She made a name for herself as a progressive politician in her country, then retired from politics to marry the aging king."

Addison looked at the empty chair Lydia had occupied. "She's a queen?"

"Dowager. Her son is king now. It's a purely ceremonial title for a small country most people can't find on a map. In any case, her departure doesn't bode well for the Council." The woman picked up her wine glass and turned to the person on the other side of her.

Addison sipped her own wine. That wasn't necessarily a bad thing. Discussions eventually returned to more mundane topics, and the rest of dinner was uneventful.

Gathered in Paige and Graham's room once more, Addison began with the most important question. "This helps us, right?"

"Yes," Graham said. "I don't know what went down between those women, but it absolutely helps for us."

"Do we need to change anything?" Devon said.

"No," Paige said. "Tinker and Jane are timing their arrival based on zero three thirty—it's too late to move the timeline. But it does mean that everyone will likely have been asleep longer and there will be less of a chance of running into any late-night partiers. Plus, Tatiana will be distracted."

"How bad was that scene at dinner?" Addison asked. "The woman sitting next to me said they go way back."

"It was pretty bad," Connie said. "Lydia is one of the original members of the Council and one of Tatiana's oldest friends. For Lydia to object to how she's operating sends a really strong message to the other members who have turned a blind eye to Tatiana's activities."

"As long as it helps us, I don't really care," Devon said.

Addison couldn't have agreed more. Tatiana's empire needed to fall, and she would do everything in her power to make sure that happened.

"Everyone try to get some rest. Zero three thirty go time," Graham said. "Pack only the essentials to take with you—the less the better."

Paige groaned. "All those pretty clothes. I'm claiming them as an expense."

"Don't you always?" Graham asked.

Addison smiled, then thought of the blue dress she'd bought. Hmm...maybe she could fit it in her go bag—it was a seriously hot dress.

"You coming?" Devon asked.

She nodded. "Yeah. See you guys in about four hours."

Devon rested his hand on her lower back as they crossed the hall. "How are you feeling?"

"Antsy. Restless. Nervous." She pushed open the door to their room.

"Understandable." He shrugged out of his jacket and slung it over the end of the bed, then loosened the tie around his neck and unbuttoned the first two buttons of his shirt. "Want to work some of that nervous energy out?"

She stopped pacing and stared at him. Damn. Standing in the middle of the room with his tie askew and his hands in his pockets, he was eye porn. It hit her—this was probably the last chance they'd have to be together. They hadn't really discussed after.

After they rescued Braedon and Michael. After they got back to the States. After their lives returned to normal—if that ever happened. This was it for them, and she might be more anxious about that than getting Braedon out of the dungeon.

"What?" he asked when she just stared at him.

She kicked off her heels and unzipped the zipper at the back of her dress, letting it slide off her shoulders, over her hips to the floor.

"Addy?"

"Devon?"

"What are you doing?"

"Taking my clothes off. What are you doing?"

His Adam's apple bobbed, and he licked his lips. His gaze trailed down her body. "Watching you take off your clothes."

"Are you just going to watch?"

He slid his tie over his head and let it drop. "You gonna take your bra off?"

"I think I'll wait until you're caught up."

She laughed when he pulled his shirt off without unbuttoning it, popping a few buttons in the process, and stripped out of his pants. He forgot about his shoes and fell over when his feet got tangled in the fabric.

"Oh, you think this is funny." Free of his clothes, he leapt up and tackled her to the bed.

Addison shrieked as they hit the bed and bounced.

"Shh." He covered her mouth with his hand. "People are going to think I'm murdering you."

"Please. Like I'm the only one screaming in this place. Besides, you're the sub—they'll think you're the one screaming."

"In that case, you should be on top." He rolled them over and centered them on the bed.

She pushed up and straddled his hips. "Now that I have you here, what should I do with you?"

"Whatever you want."

His words felt heavier than he probably intended. Devon gripped her ass and rocked her hips, reminding her she shouldn't read anything into his comment other than a sexual invitation.

Bending forward, she flicked his nipple with her tongue before sucking it into her mouth and biting it.

He groaned and rolled his hips under her, rubbing his erection against her cleft. The friction was delicious, and she rocked against him. His hands traveled up her sides and around her back to unclasp her bra and drag the straps down her arms.

She stood over him and shimmied out of her underwear. When he realized what she was doing, he pushed his boxers down his hips and kicked free. His erection rested against his stomach and bounced when she licked her lips. Well, someone was happy to see her.

Straddling him once more, she was centered on him, his length splitting her. Devon sat up and pulled her tight, crushing her breasts against his chest. His rigid cock slid against her clit, sending sharp tingles straight to her nipples.

He slid his hand behind her neck and held her while he devoured her mouth. Their tongues twisted together, sliding and pushing, giving and taking. It was possibly the most devastating kiss of her life. She concentrated on the feel of him—his firm lips under hers, the way his fingers tangled in her hair, the way his chest hair abraded her nipples. Committing every second to memory in case this really was the last moment she had with him.

His hands grabbed her outer thighs. "Lift up, Addy."

She rose up on her knees until she felt the tip of him nudging against her entrance. Keeping her gaze locked with his, she slid down his length, taking all of him. She inhaled sharply as she teetered on the edge of it being too much.

"Fuck. I need you to move." He pushed her hips back and forward. "You're in control here."

Addison repeated the motion, rocking back and forth. "Like that?"

"God. Yes. Just like that." He dragged his tongue up her neck. "Do you know how good you feel? So hot and slick. I can feel you squeezing around me, dragging on my dick when you move."

Her inner muscles clenched at his dirty talk.

"Fuck…when you do that—it's the sweetest fucking torture. I want it to go on forever. It's all I can do not to throw you back and fuck you hard until you come all over my cock and scream my name." He thrust up to punctuate his words.

"You have a dirty mouth," she said.

"Yeah, I do." He nipped at her bottom lip. "And you like it."

"You think so?"

"I know so. I can feel how wet you are. You got wetter when I said I wanted to fuck you hard."

She couldn't call him a liar, because she had. She was so wet she was afraid she would slide off if she moved any faster.

His thumb pressed on the hood of her clit and circled, sending throbs of pleasure through her entire body.

"Oh, fuck."

"There it is. I'm gonna suck on your tits and rub your clit until you come on my dick. Then I'm going to toss you on your back and fuck you until you come again."

She was going to. It was building fast, his words and his mouth doing almost as much for her as his cock throbbing inside her.

"You say you don't like anal, but I think you secretly do. So while I'm fucking you, I'm going to put my finger in your ass." He sucked hard on her nipple, using his teeth as well as his tongue.

"Oh! Shit!" Addison squeezed her eyes shut tight as she came. It rushed through her quickly, fueled on by his hands and his mouth.

He pulled her legs around his waist and took her to the bed, just as he promised. His grip on her ass was punishing as he pounded into her. Angling her hips, he slid a finger between her butt cheeks and pressed against her rear entry.

She arched her neck back with a soundless cry as another orgasm crashed through her. Devon braced himself on his arms and continued to thrust.

"You're so fucking sexy, Addison. Ah, shit. I'm coming." He collapsed onto his elbows and dropped his head in the crook of her neck, shuddering.

His back heaved under her hands.

"I'm going to need a minute," he said. "I swear, every time with you feels like I might actually explode. Like I'm going to come so hard the top of my head blows off. The big head, not the little head. Although that does blow. Hard. I know I'm babbling, but fuck, I want you to know how good it is."

She grinned against his shoulder.

"I can feel you laughing at me," he said.

"I swear I'm laughing with you."

"Liar." He kissed her jaw and pulled out. "I'm going to clean up, then we should get some rest—even if it's only for an hour or so."

"Okay." She tilted her head to watch him walk away, completely unabashed with his nudity.

The toilet flushed and water ran. Devon came out and snagged his boxers from the floor. "Your turn."

"Thanks." She sprang up from the bed, weirdly energized. Usually after sex, she had to force herself to get up and clean up, but tonight it was as if the sex had recharged her batteries.

Wrapping a towel around her after a quick shower, she walked out of the bathroom and said, "I'm going to—"

Devon was fast asleep, one arm above his head, the other resting on his chest.

Addison drank in the sight of him. It was the first time she'd had to really study him without worrying about him or someone else catching her.

The next few days were going to be insane. If everything went well and Braedon didn't need too much medical attention, she'd have no commitments, no work to report to. She had plenty of time before she really had to worry about finding a job. She could spend that time in Charleston and really get to know him outside of this craziness.

Who knew? They might not have anything in common, but it would be stupid not to even try.

CHAPTER 20

"Devon?"

He jerked and sat up. Addison was several steps away from the side of the bed. "Shit. Did I swing at you?"

She shook her head. "No."

"Then why are you over there?"

"Uh…I've always done it. Ever since I was a little girl."

He inhaled sharply, remembering some of the things Braedon had confided in him. "Your dad used to drink."

"Yeah."

"He was violent?" Braedon had never shared that.

"Not on purpose, but he was a belligerent drunk and could be combative. We learned to duck if we had to wake him up."

He swung his legs over the side of the bed. "Damn, Addy. I'm sorry."

She shook her head. "Not your fault."

"Maybe not." He held out his hand, breathing a sigh of relief when she stepped between his legs with no hesitation. "Still sucks you had to learn that lesson."

Rubbing his shoulders, she asked, "Why did you ask if you woke up swinging?"

"I've done it once or twice. Usually when I've had a nightmare."

"Did you have any last night?"

"No." He shook his head. "I don't think I dreamed at all, actually."

Most nights, he woke up once or twice from his dreams, but now that he thought about it, he didn't recall waking up at all the last few nights.

"What time is it?" he asked.

"Three," she said.

"Shit. I meant to be up half an hour ago." He pushed her back to stand. "I need to prep the bags. Check the gear."

"It's done."

"You already packed?"

"Yes. You should probably double-check to make sure I didn't miss anything, though."

The vests were ready to go, backpacks stacked on top, and weapons on the table. "What time did you get up? Why didn't you wake me up?"

Addison shrugged. "I couldn't sleep. I was too keyed up so I did some yoga and prepped everything."

"You should have woken me up." He unzipped one of the bags, saw her clothes, and closed it back up.

"There wasn't that much to do, and it kept me busy."

"Thanks." He grabbed a pair of black cargo pants and a long-sleeved shirt from the bag, dressing quickly. After lacing his boots up, he checked the weapons and magazines. She had everything ready to go.

Sitting on one end of the couch, he watched her pace back and forth. She was dressed in exactly the same clothes—black cargo pants, long-sleeved shirt, boots. She'd braided her hair and her face was devoid of makeup.

He had an overwhelming urge to have "the talk." The one where he told her he was falling for her and wanted her to come back to Charleston with him. That he wanted to explore this thing between them because, as intense as the situation was, they had a connection separate and apart from the mission and their pretend relationship.

The timing sucked. They were—he checked his watch—nine minutes from go time, so he shoved the urge down and hoped he'd have an opportunity before they got back to the U.S.

"Add? You good? You want to go over anything?" he asked.

She shook her head. "I'm good. Lights go out. Right out the door, down the hall and stairs, across the foyer to the sitting room, back corner, more stairs to the dungeon. Free Braedon and Michael, through the wall, through the tunnel, onto the boat. Speed away."

He smiled at her recitation of the mission. They hadn't done a dry run, not that they could, but they'd talked it through and discussed any possible issues.

"And if we encounter anyone?"

"Subdue as a first option."

Devon checked his watch again. "Let's gear up so we're not doing this in the dark."

She nodded and moved to her equipment, sliding on her vest and settling it over her shoulders.

He did the same, then strapped a throat mic around his neck and inserted the earpiece. "Comms check," he whispered.

"Read you loud and clear, Cactus." It sounded like Graham was standing next to him, whispering in his ear.

"I keep forgetting to ask—why Cactus?" Addison asked.

"High altitude, low opening jump in Texas. A few of us missed the LZ. I landed in a cactus patch."

She grinned. "Really? Were you the only one?"

"Yup. I was picking spines out of my ass and legs for days." He slung the backpack over his shoulders, then looped his arm through his rifle sling and adjusted the weight so it hung properly.

"Standby," Graham said.

Devon slid a hand behind Addison's neck and kissed her quickly. "Thirty minutes, we can all breathe easy."

She grasped his wrist and squeezed.

"Ten seconds," Graham said.

"NVGs," Devon said.

She nodded and settled the helmet over her head, snapping the strap under her chin.

~

*A*ddison counted down in her head, closing her eyes when she got to five. She'd kept the lights low, knowing their eyes would have to adjust to the darkness, even with the night vision goggles. That was one of the reasons they were waiting a minute after Angie cut the power. She opened her eyes to complete darkness.

"Sixty seconds," Graham said.

"Turn on your NVGs," Devon said.

Adjusting the goggles over her eyes, she fumbled with the switch on the back of the helmet. Devon's fingers found hers and flipped the unit on. An eerie green glow formed, and she blinked at how bright it was.

"Hang on, it's too bright," he whispered.

Why did darkness always lead people to whisper? Seconds ago, they'd been speaking at a normal volume.

The light dimmed until it no longer felt like it burned her retinas.

"Better?" he asked.

"A little more. Sorry—I should have checked them before now."

"Can't imagine you've had too many opportunities to use them," he said.

"A few, but not regularly."

"Good?"

"Perfect."

He nodded. "Let's move to the door."

"Fifteen seconds."

He slowly turned the door handle and eased the door open so it barely touched the frame.

She shouldered her rifle at a low ready, closed her eyes, and took a deep breath.

"Go."

The door swung open silently, and he checked the corridor before slipping out. Addison followed and spotted Graham and Paige a few steps ahead of them down the hall.

The castle was silent, the occasional jangle of equipment the only sounds. That and the blood rushing in her ears as adrenaline increased her heart rate.

Graham paused at the base of the stairs, checking left and right before raising his hand and signaling them forward. They crossed the foyer and sitting room to the back corner and hidden staircase.

Paige pushed on the release mechanism next to the door. The click of the latch echoed like a shotgun blast in the silence. Addison turned and scanned the room behind them. Everything was still. And creepy, seen through a green glow.

Maybe her post-retirement plan should be to open a haunted house where everything was silent and dark. Nothing would pop out at people to scare them. Maybe the occasional gust of air, a creak or moan, a light brush as they passed something. Their imaginations would do the rest of the work.

"Addison," Devon whispered.

He waited beside the door and tilted his head, indicating she should go through. The stone stairs were much easier to traverse in her boots than the heels she'd been in the previous time. She hit the bottom and crossed over to Paige and Graham, standing in front of the cells.

The doors to the cells were still closed. Braedon was asleep, or drugged, on the cot in his cell. It didn't matter that it was glass and carpet instead of shackles and dirt. They were cells, and they were in a dungeon.

"What's wrong?" she asked.

"The locks should have released when the power went out as a safety precaution," Paige said.

"Ange, you there?" Graham asked.

"I'm here."

"The cell doors aren't open."

"Hang on, let me check."

Addison glanced over at Devon, keeping watch at the base of the stairs.

"They aren't locked," Angie said. "Did you try the handle?"

Paige turned the metal handle on the door, and it swung open. Everyone stared at Graham.

"What? I expected the doors to pop open. That's what happens in the movies," he said.

"Did he just—?" Angie asked.

"Yes. Yes, he did," Paige said.

Devon laughed softly. "This is gold."

"Shut it—all of you." Graham moved to the other cell.

Addison slid past Paige into Braedon's cell and knelt beside the bed. She lifted the goggles and turned on the red dongle light hanging from the center of her vest. It didn't cast a lot of light, but it would let Braedon see her.

"Braedon." She shook his shoulder. "Wake up."

His eyes fluttered, and he groaned and let out a little snore but didn't wake up. She didn't know how they'd been drugging him or with what, but hopefully it was something mild. Time for drastic action.

"Yo, dork butt. Wake up. Dad is on his way up, and you need to sneak your girlfriend out."

He sat up quickly. "Shit. You gotta go."

Shaking his head like he was trying to get something out of his face, he blinked rapidly and squinted at her, even with the minimal light.

"Addison?"

"Hey, baby brother." Her voice broke at the end, and she swallowed hard.

"Where am I? What are you doing here?"

"You're in a dungeon, in a castle in Crimea. I'm here to get you home."

"There was a house. A target. It exploded. Michael. They had Michael, too."

"I'll explain everything when we're out of here. Michael's next door. We're getting him out, too. Can you stand?"

He rested his head in his hands. "I don't know. Weak. They keep giving me something—in the water, I think—had to drink."

A loud bang sounded, and she stood, stepping out of the cell to see what it was.

Graham had Michael out of his cell, supporting him under one arm with another wrapped around his waist. He looked as weak as Braedon.

Devon pushed her back into the cell. "We need to get him up. Tinker and Jane are opening up the passageway."

"Won't someone hear?" she asked.

He shook his head. "Between the ocean and the thick walls, hopefully not, but we need to be ready to go as soon as they come through."

"I need help supporting him," she said.

"I got him." He slung his rifle to his side. "Hey, Foster. I need to get you up."

Braedon raised his head. "Nash? Shit, man. Did you drag my sister into this?"

If he wasn't so weak, she'd have smacked him upside the head.

"Pfft. I didn't drag her into anything—she insisted." He leaned down and swung Braedon's arm around his neck. "Up." He grunted as he lifted him off the cot.

Addison left the cell and waited just outside the door, watching the brick wall shake as dust and small rocks fell. A few bricks tumbled out of the wall, followed by several more. In a sudden burst of dust, the wall collapsed, revealing Tinker on the other side, holding a metal battering ram.

"Y'all ready to go or what?"

She smiled. Hell, yes, she was ready to go. Devon and Braedon passed her, following Graham and Michael. She and Paige brought up the rear, covering their six as they escaped through the tunnel.

Large chem lights on the ground lit the way, and she flipped up the NVGs. There was no need to hide the fact that the tunnel was used for the escape. The huge, gaping hole gave that away. It took significantly longer to reach the mouth of the tunnel than it had the day prior.

Had it really been just yesterday that they had been there? It felt like years ago, not mere hours.

A sleek go-fast boat waited for them close to the shore, Jane at the wheel. Tinker tossed the battering ram into the boat and hauled himself over the side.

Braedon stumbled in the water and went to his knees, taking Devon with him. Addison gasped, watching them struggle to find their footing, but they managed to gain their feet. Devon hefted Braedon up and Tinker pulled him in the boat. Graham did the same with Michael.

"Ladies," Graham called. "Your turn."

It wasn't the most graceful entrance she'd ever executed, but she made it into the boat without landing on anyone.

Once everyone was on board, Jane throttled the engines and turned the boat west, heading into the Black Sea. She heard the deep thrum of helicopter blades over the roar of the engine and splash of waves. Her heart leapt in her throat, and she scanned the sky overhead. Floodlights from three hovering helicopters illuminated the castle. Men fast-roped down to the courtyard and roof.

She exchanged glances with Paige. The helicopters weren't for them—it was the raid on the castle. Tsarevna was going down.

Addison scrambled up and followed Braedon and Michael into the small hold of the boat, doing her best to ignore her somersaulting stomach. Mats and sleeping bags were laid out for them.

Braedon sat on one of the mats, shivering. She set her rifle down and took off all her gear.

"Take off your clothes and get in the sleeping bag." She pulled at the hem of his shirt.

He slapped her hands away. "I can do it."

"Don't be stubborn," she said.

Braedon stripped out of the white T-shirt and gray sweat pants and slid into the sleeping bag. Michael took off his pants, since those were the only things that got wet, and slid into the other bag.

It hit her suddenly. Braedon was safe. He was alive and safe. They were all alive and safe. She plopped down on her butt, covered her face with her hands, and burst into tears.

"Ah, shit."

Braedon pulled her closer and wrapped her in a tight hug. She wrapped her arms around his neck and squeezed tight. She might never let him go.

"You're choking me," he said.

"I don't care."

"You came all this way to rescue us and now you're going to kill me? Doesn't make a lot of sense."

"I hate you."

"No, you don't," he whispered.

She shook her head against his neck. "No, I don't."

Doing her best to breathe through her nose, she closed her eyes. A full-body shudder shook her.

"You going to be sick?" he asked.

"Yup." She dashed out of the hold and hung her head over the side of the boat, emptying the contents of her stomach into the dark sea.

A rough blanket draped over her, and a large hand rubbed her back.

"Christian picked up some anti-motion sickness medicine," Devon said. "Let me know when you think you can keep it down."

She nodded through a stomach spasm and groaned, grabbing onto his hand that rested on the rail. Wiping her mouth with her sleeve, she pressed her forehead against his arm and chest.

"Think you can lie down with your brother and take some medicine?"

She nodded and let him lead her back into the cabin, thankful that for once she didn't have to take care of herself.

CHAPTER 21

"Paige, Graham, can you come to the cockpit?" Turner, TLC's pilot, asked over the intercom.

They both unbuckled and sidestepped to the front of the C-12 they'd chartered to fly them from Ukraine to Germany.

Devon brushed his thumb over Addison's cheek. "Addy, wake up."

She inhaled and yawned. "Have we landed?"

"Soon."

Paige and Graham returned to their seats.

"We're being met," Graham said.

Addison sat upright. "By who?"

"Some ambulances and the U.S. Air Forces Europe Commander," Graham said.

"This should be interesting," she said.

The small plane landed with a screech as the tires touched down on the runway.

"German customs and immigration is getting on first," Turner said over the intercom.

Addison looked at Graham, wide-eyed. "Our passports."

"I have them," Paige said. "I sent all our information ahead.

Everything is in order—this is just a formality."

The plane stopped, and the engines shut down. Harrison exited the cockpit and opened the plane's door, lowering the steps, then moving back out of the way for the German officials to board.

"*Guten tag. Sprichst du Deutsch?*" the first man asked.

"*Ich spreche ein bisschen,*" Paige said.

Paige handed over the stack of passports while answering questions in a mix of broken German and English. In the middle of their conversation, a three-star general boarded, followed by an Air Force Chief Master Sergeant. It was getting crowded on their little plane.

Graham stood from his seat and reached around Paige with his hand outstretched. "Lieutenant General."

He took his hand and shook it. "Colonel Graham."

"Just Mister Graham now," Graham said. "Thank you for meeting us—that wasn't necessary."

"Unfortunately, it was. I'm here to escort you to Ramstein Air Base for debriefing." His name tape said Bucton.

"Excuse me? For what reason?" Graham asked.

"It's neutral territory. Between the Naval Criminal Investigative Service, the Air Force Office of Special Investigations, the CIA, the FBI, and the CENTCOM Commander breathing down my neck, it was the best solution I could come up with."

"I'm going to the hospital with my brother," Addison said.

"We're all going to the hospital," Graham said. "It's as neutral as the base is."

"There's no cleared facility at the hospital," General Bucton said.

"We're civilians—you don't need a cleared facility to debrief us," Paige said.

"The Fosters and Drake are still active duty. As such, we have jurisdiction."

"According to the Department of Defense, Senior Chief Foster and Petty Officer Drake are dead," Devon said. "I'm not sure anyone has jurisdiction."

The general crossed his arms and stared at Devon and Graham. "Major Foster is still active duty and does fall under my jurisdiction."

Addison stood and matched the general's pose. "Well, sir, I'll tell you the same thing I told the last general who stood in the way of me and my family—court-martial me."

Devon couldn't fight the grin that tugged at his mouth and looked down. He thought she was going to tell him to fuck off. It was a completely inappropriate time to get turned on.

"I'm going to the hospital with my brother," she said. "So you can either let me go, and I'll answer anyone's questions after I'm reassured my brother is physically cared for, or you can arrest me. Which, given the fact that I and everyone on this plane brought him and Michael Drake back from the dead, isn't going to look good for you or the Air Force once it hits social media."

The general's lips pinched together. "I'll inform everyone of the change of venue." He spun and pushed passed the chief master sergeant, then stomped down the stairs.

The chief turned and winked at Addison. "Major Foster." She followed the general down the stairs at a more sedate pace.

The German official handed Paige the stack of passports. "Welcome to Germany."

"I hope coming back from the dead is easier than getting to the hospital."

Everyone turned and looked at Michael Drake.

Devon grinned. "Here's hoping."

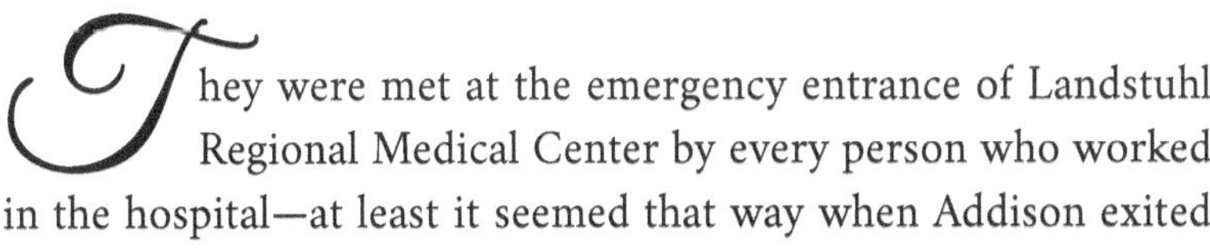

They were met at the emergency entrance of Landstuhl Regional Medical Center by every person who worked in the hospital—at least it seemed that way when Addison exited the large SUV they'd ridden in. The crowd threatened to swallow her whole as the team of doctors and nurses pulled the two gurneys out of the ambulance.

"Addison!" Devon grabbed her arm and pulled her from the throng of people.

She looked over her shoulder at him, then back at Braedon, disappearing through the automatic doors.

"Let them take care of him. They aren't going to let you in the examination room anyway," he said.

She vibrated with tension and anxiety.

He rubbed her upper arm. "I know it's hard to let him go, but he's going to be fine."

Her shoulders sagged. "I really don't want to let him out of my sight. I feel like if I can't keep eyes on him, he's going to disappear again, and this will all turn out to be a dream."

Devon pulled her close and wrapped his arms around her shoulders. "I know, but let the docs do their job. Besides, there's a shit ton of people that want to talk to us. You probably most of all."

"Fuck," she said under her breath.

"Yeah. Come on. Let's see what Paige and Graham have coordinated." He released her shoulders and followed behind the crowd. She threaded her fingers in his and caught his surprised glance at their hands. Had she crossed some kind of line? Had he left everything back at the castle? His tightening grasp eased some of her worry and she stayed close to his side.

Lieutenant General Bucton was waiting for them inside the reception area when they entered. "Major Foster, Colonel Jefferson and General Dixon would like to speak with you."

"They're here? For the debrief?"

She couldn't keep the panic from her voice. How the hell did Colonel Jefferson and the CENTCOM Commander get there so fast? Paige had only made the call a few hours ago.

General Bucton shook his head. "No, this isn't part of the

debriefing—they asked to set up a video teleconference to speak to you separately. I told them you'd be available in two hours. You'll be debriefed first, but if nothing else, this will give you a reason to end the debrief."

She cocked her head, wondering at the sudden change of attitude. "Thank you," she said.

"I apologize for earlier," he said. "Chief Tiller reminded me of everything you'd been through the past few months. I'm sorry that I forgot to take that into consideration."

"I—Thank you. And thank Chief Tiller for me."

"I will. If you're still in the debriefing, I'll grab you for the VTC. I assume Mr. Graham and Ms. Davis will want to be present," General Bucton said.

"Yes," she said.

"And me," Devon said.

The general's gaze flicked to their entwined hands. "Of course. Offices are set aside on the second floor for the debriefings. Mr. Graham and Ms. Davis have already gone up. The VTC will be in the Commander's suite on the same floor." He pulled his cell phone out of his pocket. "Excuse me."

"You ready to go up?" Devon asked.

"May as well."

The second floor was bustling with activity. More than a few junior enlisted airmen looked like they wanted to set everything on fire and run for the nearest exit. Graham waved to them from across the room, and Addison followed Devon to him.

"Addison, this is Colonel Tarek," Graham said. "She's the Medical Group Commander and will be overseeing Braedon and Michael's treatment."

"It's nice to meet you," Colonel Tarek said. "We're going to take very good care of your brother and Petty Officer Drake."

"Thank you," Addison said. "When will I be able to see Braedon?"

"Soon," the doctor said. "We're going to run a full panel of tests to try to determine what drugs they ingested and whether there will be any long-term side effects. We're trying to figure out a way to have them separated from the rest of the patients so you all can have some privacy while you're here."

"Thank you," Graham said.

"If you'll excuse me, I need to order those tests and give directions to their care teams. If you run into *any* problems, please have someone page me. I'll make sure my staff knows I'm available to you while you're here."

Paige approached from the elevator bank. "I sent Turner and Harrison to pick up rental cars. General Bucton is pushing through base access for everyone so we can come and go when we need to. Angie made hotel reservations for us not far from the base."

"Let's get these debriefings over with," Graham said.

Addison leaned some of her weight against Devon. "This is going to take forever."

"It shouldn't," Paige said. "Everyone will be debriefed individually, but all the agencies will be represented during each debrief."

"How did you manage that?" Devon asked.

"I told them it was that, or they could wait for the statement from our lawyer," Graham said.

Devon turned to Addison. "Do you want someone in there with you?"

"No. I've got it. Thanks, though."

She caught the slight downturn twitch of his lips. Was he disappointed she didn't want him with her? She'd appreciate the support, but it would be faster if they were interviewed separately. Before she could agree to having him in the interview, someone called her name from across the office and motioned for her to follow.

With a parting glance over her shoulder, she left Devon to sit through the debriefing by herself.

*D*evon sighed and scrubbed his hands over his face. The agents questioning him had been thorough but brief. If he had to guess, it was because they wanted to get through the non-essential people so they could join Addison or Graham's debrief. They'd confirmed his suspicions when half of them had gone into the office with Addison and half into the office with Graham.

He checked his watch. Addison had gone in ahead of him, and he'd been waiting for almost half an hour. Their VTC was scheduled to start in fifteen minutes.

The disappointment when she'd turned down his offer to sit through her interview with her had surprised him. He hadn't expected any other response and was having a hard time figuring out why it had upset him so much. She was so independent and capable, it was hard to figure out how to help her—to be there for her. Maybe because it would be nice to be needed for once.

The office door opened, and Addison exited, pulling it closed behind her and leaning against it.

Giving her a moment to recover, he waited for her to notice him. She pushed away from the door and saw him when she turned toward the reception area.

"Hey. Are you waiting for me?" she asked.

"Of course. I wanted to make sure you were okay."

She sat in the seat next to him. "Thanks. You didn't have to do that."

"I know." He knew. He hadn't even been sure she would appreciate it but couldn't leave without checking on her. "Besides, the VTC starts soon. I wanted to be able to pull you and Graham out if I had to."

Her head dropped back to rest on the chair back. "Ugh. When is this going to end?"

"Soon. I'm going to grab Graham." He knocked on the other

office door and pushed it open. Everyone turned to glare at him. Except Graham, who looked bored. "We have the VTC in ten minutes. Figured you'd need to take a piss first."

Graham pushed away from the table. "Good call. Agents. You have my lawyer's information if you have more questions."

Devon smirked as all the agents grumbled, but didn't try to stop him from leaving. "How bad did you screw with them?"

"Eh. Not too bad. They're just doing their jobs, but holy shit, are they new. They missed a lot of information simply because they didn't know to ask it."

"And you didn't coach them?"

Graham scoffed. "Hell, no. Not my circus anymore. Where're we doing the VTC?"

"Conference room down the hall," Devon said.

"I'll meet you there."

A non-commissioned officer was in the conference room when they arrived, fiddling with the equipment. "I'll have this up for you in just a moment," he said.

"No rush," Addison said. "In fact, if you can't get it to work at all, that would be great."

The NCO froze and stared at her, mouth slightly open. "Uh…"

"I'm kidding. Kind of."

"Uh, okay. The other side is going to dial in. All you have to do is press the green button on the remote." He pointed at the button and set the remote at the head of the table. "I'll leave you to it."

They watched him retreat, holding the door open for Graham and Paige to join them. Graham motioned for Addison to take the chair at the head of the table, but she shook her head, taking the seat on the other side of Devon. Graham shrugged and took the chair.

The VTC chimed and a notification popped up on the screen.

"Ready?" Devon asked.

"I guess," Addison said.

Devon pointed the remote at the computer and pushed the

green button. Two officers, a colonel and a four-star general, appeared on the screen. Behind them sat three other people in uniform. It was impossible to see their service affiliation on the screen, but they all held notebooks in their laps.

"Hello," one of the officers in front said. "I'm Colonel Jefferson. I was the Detachment Commander when Senior Chief Foster and Petty Officer Drake were assumed killed in action. This is General Dixon, CENTCOM Commander."

"Aiden Graham, owner and CEO of The Leonidas Corporation. Paige Davis, COO of The Leonidas Corporation. Devon Nash, security specialist for TLC and, of course, Addison Foster, Senior Chief Foster's sister." Graham indicated each of them in turn.

The colonel nodded as they were introduced. "Major Foster. Good to see you again."

"Colonel." She didn't return the sentiment.

"I want to begin by apologizing," Colonel Jefferson said. "We should have taken your concerns more seriously, Major Foster. We should have believed you."

"I want to thank you for your perseverance," General Dixon said. "And to thank you and The Leonidas Corporation for your actions and dedication. They will not go unrecognized."

Addison stiffened next to Devon. He touched her fingers and shook his head slightly. She clenched her jaw but clasped his hand in return.

"We have some questions, if you don't mind," General Dixon said.

"Of course," Graham said.

"The most pressing question is, do you have any information on the other team members that were declared killed in action? Is there any chance any of them are also alive?" the general asked.

"We don't," Paige said. "The only reason we had definitive information on Foster and Drake was because Michael Drake managed to get access to a phone and call his parents."

"Do you know how he was able to do that?" Colonel Jefferson asked.

"No," Graham said. "But we haven't asked. I'm sure it will come up during his debriefing with the Joint Personnel Recovery Agency once he's reintegrated back in the U.S."

"Why didn't you come to us?" General Dixon asked.

Graham laced his fingers together and rested his hands on the table in front of him. "Several reasons. The primary one being your inability to operate against a private citizen in a sovereign country quickly and expeditiously."

"Mr. Graham, we are the U.S. Central Command. We are the very definition of expeditious," the general said.

"With all due respect, General—"

"Graham." Addison leaned forward. "The reason I didn't contact you is because I didn't trust you. I spent weeks trying to get someone—anyone—to believe me instead of dismissing me as a hysterical, hormonal woman. The Drakes were dismissed when they did reach out after being contacted by their son. So instead of explaining why we didn't contact you, why don't you explain why we should have."

Her voice vibrated with anger and her grip on Devon's hand was punishing. He'd never been more awed by another person in his entire life.

"You had an obligation—"

She was having none of it. "I had an obligation to find my brother. That is the only obligation I had. Unless you requested this VTC to tell me I'm being court-martialed, I need to check on my brother."

Colonel Jefferson wiped a hand over his mouth, but neither man said anything.

"Have a good day, gentlemen." She picked up the remote and ended the call, then folded her arms on the table and dropped her head into them. "Fuck. I may get court-martialed after all."

"Nah." Paige stood and walked toward the door. "You're pretty much untouchable right now. We'll give them some time to cool down and then we'll set up another VTC to walk them through everything that happened. They just want answers—they don't have to get them from you."

Addison raised an arm and gave a thumbs-up but didn't lift her head.

Graham squeezed Devon's shoulder on the way out of the conference room.

"You okay?" Devon asked once the door closed and they were alone.

She raised her head. "Yeah. I just need everything to settle down and not be so chaotic."

Speaking of settling down... "What would you say to taking some time off once all this craziness dies down?"

She propped her head on her hand. "That's the general idea. I'm going to need some serious downtime once Braedon gets back to the U.S."

He rubbed the back of his neck and turned his seat to face her fully. She didn't understand what he was asking. "What I mean is—"

A knock on the door interrupted him. It opened, and the NCO from earlier leaned the upper half of his body in the room. "Major Foster, Colonel Tarek asked me to inform you they're moving your brother to a room and to ask if you want me to take you there."

Addison popped up from her chair. "Yes!" She looked at Devon. "I'll catch up with you in a little bit?"

He leaned back in his chair. "Sure. Yeah. Of course."

"Thanks." She kissed him on the cheek and rushed to the door, disappearing through it.

He'd have plenty of time later to ask her to take time off with him.

CHAPTER 22

Devon handed his ID card to the guard at the front of the ward. The hospital at Landstuhl had shut down the entire floor and tightened security with their arrival. It wasn't every day a private security company rescued a service member presumed killed in action and showed up on the doorstep of the largest U.S. military hospital in the region.

The guard checked his name against the authorized roster and waved him through. Everyone was trying to keep the news of Braedon and Michael's rescue quiet as long as possible. The good thing about being overseas was the lack of press coverage, but Addison, Braedon, and Michael were scheduled for a military flight back to D.C. early the next morning. No doubt the media circus would start soon after they landed.

The ward was one of the smaller ones, and Braedon and Michael were the only patients. With the drawdowns in Iraq and Afghanistan, the hospital had more space and was able to accommodate their request for privacy and security. Devon stopped first at the room on the left, knocking on the door.

"Come in."

He pushed open the door to Michael Drake's room and found him pacing. "Hey. How's it going?."

"Oh, good. I thought you were one of the nurses." He started doing walking lunges across the room.

"They yell at you for exercising?" Devon asked.

"Yeah. But I can't lie in that bed. I lay in a bed for weeks, barely able to stand for more than a few minutes. Right now, I'm thinking I might learn how to sleep standing up."

Devon grinned. "You get a chance to talk to your family yesterday?"

He stopped lunging and nodded. "I did. That was...fuck, that was harder than I expected. My mom just cried the entire time. My dad held it together a little better, but not much."

"They meeting you in D.C.?"

"They're flying there tonight. They want to be at the hospital when I arrive. Not big on having to stay at the hospital, but the docs said they want to run more tests—MRI, EKG, EEG, LMNOP—who knows what else. Lot of debriefing, and I'm guessing lots of time with the shrinks."

"No doubt. Let us know if you need anything while you're there."

"I will, thanks."

Devon turned to leave the room.

"Hey."

He turned back, and Michael approached with his hand outstretched.

"I already told your boss, but thanks for pulling us out of that hell. Thanks for listening to my parents and not thinking they were crazy."

Devon took his hand. "Anytime."

He left the room, pulling the door closed behind him, and crossed the hall to Braedon's room. As expected, Braedon wasn't lying abed either but at least he wasn't doing walking lunges while on his video call.

"I get that you want to share the good news, Mom, but you can't tell Aunt Linda." He lifted his chin at Devon when he saw him.

"Who's that? Is that Addison?"

"No, it's a friend of mine."

Devon motioned over his shoulder, asking if he should go. Braedon shook his head and waved him into the room.

"Why does he get to know but I can't tell family? She's my sister."

"One, because he was on the rescue team. And two, because Aunt Linda has never kept a secret in her entire life."

"That's not true," his mom said.

"You remember that trip to Disney you and Dad surprised us with for our twelfth birthday?"

"Yes..."

"Aunt Linda told us a month ahead of time."

"No, she didn't."

"Yes, Mom. She did."

"Oh. Now that I think about it, your reactions did seem a little fake."

"Exactly. The Navy will make an official statement once we're back in the States. It's two days—you can talk to her about it then."

"Is that why Addison didn't tell us what she was doing?"

Braedon sat on the chair next to the bed. "Would you have believed her if she had?"

"I..."

Devon heard her sigh from his position by the door.

"No," she said. "We all thought she just couldn't accept your death and was imagining what she was feeling. You have to understand, Braedon. It's not that we didn't want to believe her— we couldn't. The Navy told us you were dead. Couldn't tell us how or where, only that you'd been killed during a mission. Addison insisted they were wrong, and we couldn't...I..."

Her voice broke. As much sympathy as Devon felt for their mom, it pissed him off to hear her talking that way about Addison. As if she'd been a nuisance that wouldn't go away instead of a sister that had been grieving the loss of her brother.

"I understand, Mom, I do. But when we get back to the States, you and Dad need to apologize."

"I know. We will."

"Good. The doctor's here, so I need to go."

Devon glanced over his shoulder, but there was no one there. He smirked when he turned back around to see Braedon making a wrap it up motion with his hand.

"All right. I love you." His mom sounded like she was either crying or close to it.

"I love you too, Mom. I'll see you in two days. Bye." He touched the phone to end the call and stood. Walking over to Devon, he pulled him into a spine-crushing hug. "Fuck, man. It's good to see you."

Devon hugged him back. "You too, brother."

"I wasn't sure if I'd imagined it was you." He pounded him on the back a few times and pulled away. "How've you been?"

"Good. I'd ask how you've been, but…you know."

Braedon laughed and returned to the chair, collapsing into it. He tossed the phone onto the bed. "My mom has not stopped calling since this morning."

Devon took a seat at the end of the bed. "She's happy you're alive. Probably wants to reassure herself it's real."

"Yeah, I get that part. It's the part where she asks if she can tell everyone. I almost wish we hadn't told them until we were back in the U.S., but that would have been an asshole move."

"When did Addison tell them?" He hadn't seen her since the VTC two days ago. She'd stayed in the hospital instead of the hotel to be closer to Braedon.

"She didn't. She asked the general to have the military officially inform them. Kind of a reverse notification of death. I was surprised, honestly. I got the feeling she took a lot of crap from them about not believing I was dead. Me personally, I would have rubbed that shit in their faces."

He leaned forward and rested his elbows on his knees. "You've spent a lot of time with her the last week—how is she really?"

Shit. How much had she shared with Braedon? They were close, but had she told him everything?

"I don't have a before to compare it to, but she's been… focused. She wasn't going to let anything or anyone stand in the way of rescuing you."

Braedon smiled. "That sounds like Addy. Nothing will stop her once she sets her mind on something." His smile fell. "She's different, though. I don't know how to explain it, but I think my parents not believing her broke something in her. She hasn't talked to them yet. Granted, she gave me her phone so I could talk to them, but anytime I mention calling them, she has to be somewhere else."

"I don't know what to tell you about that. She didn't talk about your parents other than to say she hadn't told them what she was doing. Where is she now?"

"She went for a run. I'd have gone with her, but the doc said no."

Devon laughed. "I stopped by Michael's room, and he was doing walking lunges."

"Yeah, I don't blame him. I can't be in that bed if I don't have to."

A knock at the door interrupted them. "Come in!" Braedon called.

Paige stuck her head through the door, then pushed it fully open. "There you are," she said to Devon. "Graham has another VTC with the CENTCOM Commander in ten minutes. He wants us sitting in."

"Sure. Where is it?" Devon asked.

"Fourth floor conference room. Have you seen Addison?"

"She left about twenty minutes ago for a run," Braedon said.

"Shoot. Can you let her know your flight has been pushed up six hours? You're leaving at zero three hundred now."

"Sure," Braedon said.

"Why the change?" Devon asked. That meant he had even less time to talk to Addison than before.

Now that they weren't under fire and in a stressful situation, he wanted to hash out what came next. Whether she could take some time in Charleston after Braedon got settled? Or if she'd be okay with him taking some time in D.C. or wherever she ended up in the short-term? He wanted to talk about them being a *them* and he couldn't even call her to let her know he wanted to talk to her because Braedon had her phone.

"It puts them in earlier in the day D.C. time—less traffic between Andrews Air Force Base and Walter Reed."

"I'll let her know," Braedon said.

"Thanks." Paige checked her watch and looked at Devon. "Six minutes."

Devon stood and pulled Braedon up into a one-armed bro hug. "I'll stop by again before you guys leave."

"Thanks again. I owe you big time."

"Nah, we're even," Devon said.

Braedon looked at him like he was crazy. "Even for what?"

"You remember that night we were out in Virginia Beach, a couple of my old high school buddies came down to party, and we got into it with some locals?"

"Kind of...."

"My buddies decided to follow them out of the bar, and you stopped me. Told me I didn't need that kind of trouble and that if something happened, it'd go worse for me than for them."

"Okay. I still don't see how that makes us even," Braedon said.

"What I never told you is my buddies couldn't find those guys so they decided to try to find this party some girl had told them about. They wrapped their car around a pole. One died on impact, and the other died later in the hospital."

Braedon wiped a hand over his face. "Shit, man. I had no idea."

"I didn't find out until a week or so later when I talked to my younger brother. If you hadn't stopped me that night, I would have been in that car."

"Damn." Braedon looked down and shook his head. "Not to sound like a selfish asshole—I'm really sorry about your buddies—but I can't help thinking I did myself a favor."

"What do you mean?"

"Well, think about it. If I hadn't stopped you that night, you might not have been here to drag my ass out of that hellhole. So stopping you, saved me."

"Huh. Guess everything happens for a reason."

Braedon pulled him into another back-pounding hug. "Yeah, it does." He released him, suspiciously watery-eyed. "Go to your VTC before you get fired."

Devon laughed, which helped hide his own teary eyes. "I'll see you later this afternoon."

CHAPTER 23

*A*ddison pushed into Braedon's hospital room carrying a bag of sandwiches and a shopping bag from the base exchange. "Braedon? You here?"

He stepped out of the bathroom, rubbing a towel over his head. "Hey. What's in the bags?"

"Doner kebabs and iced tea in this one." She lifted the food bag. "Sweats, T-shirts, underwear, and shoes in this one."

"You're the best sister ever."

"I know. Right?" She tossed the clothes and shoes on the bed and set the doners on the table. "I figured you might be more comfortable traveling in real clothes rather than scrubs."

"Can you prop the door open?" he asked.

"Sure." She opened it and stepped on the doorstop. "Any particular reason?"

He stared at the door for a moment, like he didn't know the answer to the question. Or, more likely, he didn't want to answer the question because answering it would be admitting he felt as trapped in the hospital room with the door closed as he had in that cell.

"Got it," she said.

The tension eased from around his mouth as he sat in one of the chairs and pulled out a sandwich. He removed the foil from the plate and lifted it to his nose, inhaling deeply, a look of pure bliss on his face. "I love you so much right now."

She grinned. "I think you love me more for the food than for rescuing you."

"I love you for that too, but this is a real doner," he said around a huge mouthful of pita bread and meat. "Did you get food and clothes for Michael? I feel bad that I have you here and he doesn't get to see his family until we get to the States."

"Yes, we got him clothes and food, too. Paige took it to him."

"Thanks. I know he's as antsy as I am being cooped up here."

They dug into their sandwiches, Braedon groaning and making *nom nom* sounds the entire time. It hit her how normal it was—how familiar. Tears welled up, and she had trouble swallowing the bite she'd taken. She grabbed her iced tea and took a big sip, washing down the food.

"Hey."

She looked up at her brother, wiping his hands on a napkin.

"You okay?" he asked.

Damn it. Why did that question always unleash the floodgates? She could usually hold it together until he asked that question.

"Hey, hey, hey." He pulled her chair to his and wrapped his arms around her. "I'm safe and I'm safe because you didn't give up." He kissed the top of her head.

"I keep thinking about what might have happened."

"Stop. It didn't. There's no use thinking about it."

"I know, but it's going to be a while before I don't wake up thinking you're still missing." She dragged her nose across his scrub top and scooted her chair back over.

He looked down at the slime streak on his sleeve. "That's disgusting."

"Whatever. It's the least you deserve for all the times you tormented me when we were kids."

He gave her a baleful look, then shrugged. "All right, I know the basics of how everything came together, but how did you connect with Leonidas?"

"I didn't really. They connected with me. Devon attended your funeral"—she hooked her fingers for air quotes—"and approached me afterward." She didn't share that she'd walked out before the end.

"And Aiden Graham just happened to let you go along on the rescue mission?"

"I insisted."

Braedon smirked. "Of course you did. What else? You were there two days—no one suspected you?"

"No. Or if they did, no one let on that they did. Connie has history with the bitch that was holding you and she provided covers for us."

"Who's Connie? I haven't met her."

Addison cocked her head. "I'm not really sure who she is, to tell you the truth. All I know is she may or may not work for the government and she has some seriously shady connections."

"CIA?" he asked.

"She neither confirmed nor denied her affiliation," she said.

"Where did she go? She wasn't with you guys. Was she?"

She shook her head. "No. There was a raid on the castle immediately after we got you and Michael out. She stayed behind to coordinate that, I think."

"And you and Devon pretended to be a couple?"

She took a large gulp of her tea and made a sound of uh-huh.

Braedon studied her for several moments, and she tried not to fidget. "And it was just pretend?"

Her heart fluttered in her chest. Wasn't that the sixty-four-thousand-dollar question because she had no idea. They hadn't had a chance to talk since they'd arrived in Germany. Really, since they'd left their room in the castle.

She didn't want it to be pretend, but she also didn't want to pour her heart out to her brother without the chance to pour it out to Devon first. Maybe not pour…maybe trickle. That way, if he didn't feel the same, she could turn off the emotional tap and chalk it up to a good time had by all.

"Of course, it was pretend. It's not like you can develop a relationship with a stranger in less than a week—especially under those circumstances." Maybe she was laying it on a little thick.

"Uh-huh."

He didn't believe her, but he wasn't going to push the issue. At least not right then. He'd bring it up down the road when she least expected it in order to ambush an honest answer out of her.

Stupid twin.

"So you and Devon were pretending to be a couple. How did you find me?" he asked.

Addison froze, a fry halfway to her mouth. "You don't…?" She dropped the fry back in the container. "You don't remember seeing me?"

His brows drew together. "When?"

"She took us down there—all of us—to see you and Michael. A *preview* of the merchandise is what she called it. You were sitting on the bed in the cell. You looked really out of it, but you stared directly at me."

Braedon's shoulders slumped. "I don't remember most of it. I remember seeing the charges in the house and telling everyone to get out. I remember the explosion throwing me. I remember the heat." He ran his fingers over his eyebrows, as if making sure they were still there. "I remember a truck and a boat, but every time my mind started to clear and I could think, they drugged me."

She scooted her chair closer and took one of his hands in hers. He dropped his head to her shoulder, and she rested her head against the top of his.

"I think there was another guy with us at the beginning," he whispered.

"One of your teammates?"

"Yeah. But I'm not sure—it's all fuzzy."

"Have you talked to Michael about it? Asked him what he remembers?"

His head shook under hers.

"I think you need to," she said. "Maybe he can provide pieces you're missing, and you can provide pieces he's missing. The shrinks at Walter Reed will probably want to talk to you together at some point, plus all the debriefing you're going to do."

He lifted his head from her shoulder. "You're right. I'll talk to him on the plane."

"What is it?" He was leaving something out.

"If there was a third guy with us…where is he now? Was he given to someone else? Was he killed? Should his family know?" He shook his head. "Would they want to know?"

"That's a tough call," she said. "It would give them hope, but it might be false hope. Tell the debriefers and let them decide. At the very least, they can change his status to missing in action instead of killed in action."

Braedon bumped her with his shoulder. "How'd you get so smart?"

She smirked. "I got all the good genes."

"That's because I got all the good looks—I had to leave you with something."

Addison stuck out her tongue and crossed her eyes. He retaliated by poking her in the ribs.

A knock on the door interrupted their burgeoning wrestling match. "Am I interrupting?" A woman in uniform stood in the doorway, a stethoscope hanging around her neck. One of the nurses stood behind her, trying not to laugh.

"Hey, Doc," Braedon said. "She's picking on me. Beating up on me when I'm weak and defenseless."

The woman came into the room. "I'm sure that's exactly what happened. Up on the bed so we can get your vitals and go over some things for your transfer."

"Yes, ma'am." He stood and hopped up on the bed.

She held out her hand to Addison. "Lieutenant Colonel Justice. I was on leave through yesterday so I wasn't here when you arrived."

Addison grinned, thinking about when the doctor would have been Major Justice and how kick-ass that would have been. "Addison Foster. That one's sister."

"It's a pleasure to meet you," Colonel Justice said. "I heard about what you did. It's truly inspiring."

"I—" Addison blushed, at a loss for words. What was she supposed to say to that?

Colonel Justice smiled. "Better get used to it. People are going to want to talk to you as much as they're going to want to talk to your brother."

"I didn't really do anything."

"Bullshit!" Braedon said.

She shot him a dirty look.

"He's right," Colonel Justice said. "You didn't give up. You didn't take no for an answer. And then you traveled halfway around the world and rescued your brother from a human trafficking ring. I'd say that's more than not doing anything."

"Uh…well…thank you. I had a lot of help."

She smiled. "You're welcome."

"I'm…gonna go…do something else while you poke him." Addison pointed toward the door. "Feel free to poke him hard."

"I heard that," Braedon said.

The doctor laughed. "I'll see what I can do."

～

Addison yawned and rubbed her palms over her eyes. The worst part of military flights were the ridiculous show times. Why did they need to be at the terminal two hours before the flight? At least they were in the VIP lounge instead of the regular waiting area.

She looked up when the door opened. Paige entered the lounge, followed by Graham. The door closed behind them. It was just them.

Her heart plunged, and that uncomfortable sense of disappointment roiled her stomach. She plastered on a big smile.

"Hey. What are you guys doing here?"

"We're on our way to the airport and wanted to say goodbye one last time," Paige said.

Addison stood and hugged her. "Thank you for everything. I know I've said it already, but there's no way I'll ever be able to thank you enough."

Paige squeezed her and leaned back. "You know...since you'll officially be out of the Air Force in a couple of weeks, TLC is hiring. I can put in a good recommendation."

Addison laughed. "Thanks, but after talking to Braedon this afternoon, I think I'm going back to school to get my doctorate and actually put my degree to use."

"What's your degree in?"

"Psychology."

"Well, you've seen how crazy we all are," Paige said.

Addison laughed again. "Fair point. Are the rest of the guys stopping by?" She didn't want to come right out and ask where Devon was.

"They left about two hours ago. They didn't say goodbye?"

He left. He was gone, and he didn't even bother to say goodbye. She fought to control her breathing. "No, but they might have stopped here and didn't realize we were in the VIP lounge."

Paige rubbed her shoulder. "I'm sure that was it." Yeah...she didn't believe it any more than Addison did.

Graham pushed Paige out of the way and pulled Addison in for a huge bear hug, lifting her off her feet. It was exactly what she needed at that moment. Setting her back down, he said, "Take care of yourself. Call us if you need anything. *Anything*, Addison—I'm not kidding."

"I know. Thank you so much."

He kissed her on the forehead. "Let us know when you get to D.C."

"I will."

Paige and Graham said their goodbyes to Braedon and left with a wave.

Addison took a deep, shaky breath and sat back down. Guess that answered her question whether Devon felt the same way. If he did, he wouldn't have ghosted.

CHAPTER 24

*"*cording to an official Navy spokesman, both Senior Chief Petty Officer Braedon Foster and Petty Officer First Class Michael Drake are recovering with their families after their surprise rescue."*

The anchor looked at her co-anchor. "It really is a miraculous event, Jeff. I can only imagine the relief these families are feeling."

"And I understand there's a rumor that the sister of one of the SEALs took part in the rescue," the male co-anchor said.

"That's true. Senior Chief Foster's sister is an Air Force officer and was involved in the rescue. I think this nation owes this brave woman a huge debt of gratitude."

"Oh, for fuck's sake." Addison rolled her eyes and turned off the T.V., tossing the remote onto the table next to her.

She flipped aimlessly through a magazine while waiting for Braedon to return to his room. After a week of tests, debriefs, and psych appointments, they were finally moving him to out-patient treatment. Which meant he was moving into her apartment until the Navy figured out what they were going to do with him.

Throwing the magazine aside, she picked up her phone and opened the contacts app, scrolling to Devon's number. She stared at it, once again trying to talk herself into calling him. But she hated being the type of woman who couldn't take a hint, and what bigger hint was there than walking away without saying goodbye?

She hadn't said goodbye either, but she'd figured there was time, that there would be a chance—either at the hospital or the terminal—and she'd been wrong. So many *should haves* played through her mind. Should have been more proactive. Should have taken the initiative. Should have called him and asked to see him.

She should do it now, but she was too much of a chickenshit. At least this way she could pretend there was a sliver of a chance he'd call her or…something. She had a glimmer of hope.

Her last senior NCO liked to say that the answer was always no if you didn't ask the question. If she called and asked the question and he told her he wasn't interested, that hope would die, and that would hurt. Bad.

Addison touched the "edit" link. She should delete his contact. She should accept that what happened in Crimea stayed in Crimea and move on.

"Hey."

She jumped and dropped her phone, fumbling it a few times until it hit the floor. Thank God for her protective phone case.

"You good?" Braedon asked.

"Yeah. You startled me." She shoved her phone in her purse. "All done?"

"Do you know how much paperwork is involved in coming back from the dead? A lot. More than there is to join the military. But yes, I'm done until next week when I have appointments for half the day," he said.

"At least it's only one day a week now."

"True." He grabbed his small duffle bag from the end of the bed. "Did you know Mom and Dad sold all my stuff?"

She pressed her lips together. "It was one of those things we argued about, yes. Mom kept a lot of your personal stuff though—pictures, awards, and some other stuff. It's in boxes in the garage.

"What brought that up?" She followed him out of the room and down the hall, waving to the nurses at the desk as they passed.

"I'm going to need to buy a car. I don't want to take the metro right now with my face all over the news and I can't keep relying on you for a ride." They entered the elevator, and he pushed the button for the ground floor. "Do you want to go to the USO for lunch? I think they have Subway today."

"Sure." She looked at him and tilted her head.

"What? Do I have something on my face?" He brushed at his nose.

"Can you buy a car if you're officially dead?"

"Ha. Ha. My resurrection should be official in a day or two." The doors opened, and he poked her in the back. "Go."

"You can borrow my truck. The only thing I have planned next week is to go to an informational session at the college."

"Have you officially applied yet?" he asked.

She shook her head. "Not yet. I want to attend the session first. Do you want to drive or walk?"

"Let's walk. It's only five minutes, and then we can work off our lunch on the way back to the parking garage."

"Sounds like a plan."

They set off down the sidewalk, Addison lengthening her strides to keep up with Braedon. Finally, she said, "Okay, but you have to walk slower—my legs aren't as long as yours."

He slung an arm over her shoulders. "Sorry, I forgot how short you are."

"Quit it, before people think we're a couple." She stabbed her finger into his side, getting him to flinch and let go.

They'd always been mistaken for boyfriend and girlfriend as teenagers. One year, as a joke, their mom had gotten them shirts that said "he's my brother" and "she's my sister," except they wore them whenever they went somewhere together.

Braedon slowed to an easy stroll and walked the rest of the way in silence. When they arrived at the USO, he held the door for her.

"By the way, Mom and Dad are here."

Addison stopped and slowly turned to face him. "You jerk face. You set me up."

"I had to, Addy. Mom said you wouldn't take her calls."

"I'm still angry with them." She knew she sounded like a petulant child, but her parents' lack of faith had hurt.

He grasped her shoulders. "I know, but I'm going to be the asshole who plays the guilt card. I almost died, Addy. I almost disappeared into God only knows where. It puts things into perspective. Life is too short for this kind of bullshit."

She folded her arms and looked away. "It's very hard to trust them, Brae."

"I'm not asking you to trust them—you have me for that. I'm asking you to accept their apology. For me."

She couldn't ignore her parents forever. As much as she hated to admit he was right, and she would never say it out loud, he had a point.

"Fine. But if Dad's drunk, the answer's no."

"I'll give you that, but Mom said he's back in AA. *And* he's cut Uncle Steve out. Told him if he couldn't support his sobriety, Dad couldn't be around him."

Her eyebrows rose. "Really?"

"Yeah." He spun her around and pushed her forward. "Go give Mom a hug before she loses it."

She lost it anyway as soon as Addison hugged her. Her mom buried her face in Addison's hair and cried hard.

"I'm so sorry we didn't believe you," she sobbed.

"It's okay, Mom."

"It's not! You tried to tell us, and we didn't listen. We could have lost him forever!"

One day, in the far distant future, Addison would sit down

with a theoretical physicist and unpack the paradox of the possibility of losing someone you thought you'd already lost, but today all she could do was hold her mom and assure her it would be all right.

~

"That wasn't so bad, was it?" Braedon asked as they walked back to her truck.

"What? Lunch?" She shrugged. "It was fine."

"I meant Mom and Dad."

"Oh. It was good. I would have gotten there eventually," she said.

"So I was right," he said.

"You were…not incorrect."

He wrapped his arm around the back of her neck, pulling her into a loose headlock. "It kills you to admit that I'm right, doesn't it?"

She dug a finger into his ticklish spot to force him to let go.

He changed tactics and wrapped both arms around her, trapping her arms next to her body. "Say I'm right."

"No." She lunged ahead as he started to drag behind her.

"Say it!" His arms slid down to her waist, and she freed her arms, pushing at his.

"No. Let go!" she said, laughing.

"Saaaayyyy iiiiit." He slid all the way down until he lay on the ground, his arms wrapped around her ankles.

She stepped out of the circle of his arms. "What are you? Twelve?"

He popped up and grabbed his bag. "Yes. Always. Now that I have you laughing, tell me why you're so mopey."

"I'm not mopey." She dug her key fob out of her purse and unlocked her truck.

He tossed his duffle into the back seat and climbed in. "Sis, you're so mopey you could get a job at Disney as the eighth dwarf."

She glared at him as she pushed the ignition button.

"Spill it. Is it Devon?"

Something must have shown on her face because he reached over and pressed the ignition button, turning off the truck.

"Come on, tell me."

Addison leaned back against the seat and slouched down. "It wasn't…pretend. At least I didn't think it was."

"What happened?"

She shook her head and shrugged. "Nothing. Nothing happened. I didn't see him or talk to him after the first day at the hospital. I kept expecting to run into him, but I never did, and then he didn't come to the terminal to say goodbye.

"I thought…I thought we had a connection. I thought it was more than physical. I didn't have to tone it down, or hold back, or minimize my personality. I was able to be who I am without worrying about some guy's fragile ego, and it was great. I thought everything was great, but now it's…nothing."

"Have you tried calling him and asking what the fuck?" he asked.

She shook her head, picking at her cuticle.

"Why not?"

"I think not knowing is better than knowing for sure."

"What if you're wrong, and it's a big miscommunication? What if he's thinking the same thing and trying to get up the nerve to call you to ask what the fuck?"

"What if he's not?"

"Then he's a stupid fucker who doesn't deserve you anyway. But the Devon I know isn't a stupid fucker. He's a fucker who's done stupid shit, but he's not a stupid fucker. You owe it to yourself to find out for sure, Addison."

"Is this where you use your 'I almost died and life is too short' guilt trip on me?"

"Yes. This is exactly where I do that, because you know I'm right."

She smiled. "I will try to call him when we get home."

"No."

"No? You just said to find out for sure."

"Right, but you guys bumped uglies—this is a conversation you need to have in person, not over a phone. You can drop me off at the apartment and drive your happy ass to Charleston to ask him in person."

She curled her upper lip. "Don't ever say bumping uglies to me again. Ever. And...I could call him and save the gas money."

"Or...you could go in person and ask him to his face."

They had the argument the entire hour-long drive to her apartment north of Andrews Air Force Base, and in the end, she packed a few days' worth of clothes in her overnight bag and pointed her truck south.

Devon half-heartedly punched the heavy bag, trying to work up the interest to either pound on it good or give up and move on to something else. The problem was he didn't have any interest in doing anything else—hadn't since they'd left Germany.

No one had commented on his attitude—yet—but they'd been giving him enough sideways looks he knew it was coming soon.

Dani strolled into the gym and dropped her bag in front of a mirror.

He dropped his arms. "Hey. I thought you were training for a fight."

Danielle "The Dancer" Knight was Tinker's younger sister, MMA Featherweight champion contender, and all-around badass.

"I am. Graham asked me to come in and knock you guys around a bit. It's a rest day, so I figured why not?"

He hung his head. Shit. Dani was also their resident combatives instructor. Her rest day workouts were usually some of their toughest and more than one of them ended up puking.

"Yaaaayyy," he said.

She smirked and bounced around on the mat a little. "Since you're here and warmed up, you can go first."

"Lucky me." He pulled off the boxing gloves and threw them in the box along the wall. He kicked off his shoes and peeled off his socks, joining her on the mat. Bouncing on the balls of his feet, he stretched his neck from side to side.

Fuck. He was about to get his ass handed to him. No one ever beat Dani. Except Tinker, and that was only because he picked her up like a sack of flour and hauled her around. Being her brother, he could do that. No way in hell the rest of them would try it.

Fuck it. He moved quickly, pulling her into a front headlock. Next thing he knew, his knee buckled, Dani contorted her body, he was on his back, and she had him in an arm bar.

"Holy shit, Dani. What'd I do to you? Ow!" He tapped one of her legs that pinned his chest. "Give. Give."

She eased up the pressure but didn't release him. "So, what's your problem?"

"You mean other than you trying to dislocate my arm? Nothing." She increased the pressure. "Ah, fuck! What the hell?"

"I'll keep doing it until you tell me the truth. Graham called me specifically to find out what crawled up your ass."

Fucking hell. She pulled on his arm again. "Okay! Okay! I fucked up!"

"How?" she asked, increasing the force on his arm.

The woman was merciless. "Son of a—I met the woman of my dreams, and she wants nothing to do with me! Happy?"

She let him go and rolled out of range. Not that he could do anything anyway. His whole damn arm was numb.

"I heard some of the story from Christian and a lot of the story from Paige. Way more than I wanted to hear, honestly, and I don't think that's true."

Devon sat up, shaking his arm and flexing his fingers. "What? That she was the woman of my dreams or that she wants nothing to do with me?"

"That she wants nothing to do with you." She drew her knees up and rested her arms on them. "You should call her and tell her how you feel."

"It's not that easy," he said.

"Why? You don't have her number? Angie can get that."

He hooked his elbows over his knees. "I have her number. She was playing a role for the mission to get her brother back. It wasn't real."

"It was for you. I'd bet good money it was for her as well."

"I heard her, Dani. She told her brother she was just pretending."

"Dude. I don't talk to my brother about my sex life." She shuddered. "Did it ever occur to you that she told him it was pretend so she didn't have to explain the situation to him? Especially that particular situation…you know…with the rope?"

Devon pressed his lips together and narrowed his eyes. "Paige has a big mouth."

She laughed. "Can you blame her? That sounded *hawt*." She waved a hand in front of her face. "Woo, buddy. If you were anyone else, I'd be asking for a demonstration."

He pushed up and walked over to his bag, grabbing his water bottle.

"Oh, don't be mad, Devon—I'm only giving you a hard time. Kind of." She spun on her butt to face him and crossed her legs. "My point is, most women can't fake that kind of intimacy, and if that happened in front of people, I can only imagine what happened behind closed doors. *Call her* and find out the truth. What's the worst that can happen? She says she doesn't feel the same way and you're still miserable?"

Devon lowered the bottle and sighed. The little spitfire had a point. He should find out for sure. Hearing her tell Braedon it had all been a lie had felt like a physical blow. It had literally stopped him in his tracks just outside Braedon's hospital room.

He'd been excited, hearing Addison's voice. He'd planned to

talk to her in private, tell her he wanted to take some time off and go to D.C. until they figured out a long-term plan. If they had to do the long-distance thing for a while, he'd make it work, but he wanted to explore what they had together.

And then she'd told Braedon it had all been pretend for the mission. But if Dani was right, and she'd told him that because he was her brother, then Devon had walked away from her.

Fuck. She probably thought he was the biggest dick in the world.

"Damn it." He dropped his water bottle and dug out his phone.

"Atta boy!" Dani clapped once. "You do that, and I'm going to go find my next victim."

Devon put the phone to his ear and watched her leave, shaking his head. She enjoyed beating up on them a *little* too much.

The phone rang and rang, finally going to voicemail. Shit. Was she screening? Should he leave a message? Would she listen to it if she was screening? Was it weird to call and not leave a message? The call disconnected before he could make a decision.

Well, fuck. Should he call back immediately and leave a message or wait? Was it stalkerish if he called back immediately? Should he text instead? What if she had her phone on silent?

Christ. When did this shit get so difficult? He gritted his teeth and called her again, composing what he would say while it rang, and lost his entire train of thought as soon as he heard the beep.

"Addison, I think I screwed up. Actually, I know I screwed up, but I'd like to explain. Call me, please. Or text me. Whichever. I just want to know you're okay. Okay? Bye. Oh! This is Devon. Fuck."

He closed his eyes and shook his head. He was an idiot, but damn it, he was an idiot in love. As soon as he thought it, he knew it was true. He loved Addison. Had been infatuated with her for years, but knowing the real her—her strength and loyalty, her willingness to honestly be herself—he fell in love with her.

Fuck it. He was going to stalk her. He shoved his feet back into his shoes, grabbed his bag, and headed upstairs to find Angie.

"Hey, Angie, I need a favor," he said, finding her in her corner. Graham had offered to close off her area, but she'd said she liked it open. A furry face stepped out from under the desk and looked up at him.

Addison's dog. Or…Angie's dog, since she was keeping it.

"Sure, whatcha need?" Angie asked.

"Can you see if Addison has another number, other than her cell?"

"I have her home phone number," she said.

That was easy. "You do?"

"Yeah, I pulled it at the very beginning. I have her address, too. Do you want that?"

"Uh…sure." If worse came to worst, he'd drive up to D.C. and confront her in person.

Angie clapped. "Yay! You're going to get your girl and quit sulking around the office like a little boy who lost his favorite toy."

"Have I really been that bad?" he asked.

"Devon, I say this with all the sincerity in my heart, you've been a serious buzzkill since you got back."

"Well, hopefully this will fix it." He took the sticky note she held up with Addison's information on it.

"And…." She pulled a piece of paper from under her keyboard. "Damn it. Jane won the pool."

He glanced at the paper. "You guys bet on my love life?"

"Absolutely. I had you down for caving two days ago. Kind of mad you held out this long—it cost me five dollars."

"So sorry for the inconvenience."

"That's okay. You can make it up to me by staying here while you call her." She rested her chin on her fist and batted her eyes at him.

He rolled his eyes and punched in the number she'd given him, earning a big grin in return.

It rang three times. "Hello?" a male voice asked.

"Uh, Braedon?"

"No comment."

"Wait! It's Devon," he said quickly.

"Oh. Hey, man, I didn't recognize your voice."

"No problem. Is…Addison there?"

Braedon didn't answer immediately. "She should be there."

"What do you mean she should be here? Here as in Charleston, here?"

"Yeah, she left two days ago to drive down there to talk to you."

Unease rolled through Devon's stomach. "Have you tried calling her? She's not answering my calls. I figured she was screening."

"I haven't. Hang on—let me try."

He waited impatiently while Braedon tried to call her. Angie looked up at him, brows furrowed, before turning away to type furiously on her keyboard.

"She's not answering," Braedon said. "Shit. I've had a bad feeling since yesterday, but I figured it was because you'd been a dick and broke her heart. I tried TLC's main number, but no one answered."

He lowered the phone from his mouth. "Did another receptionist quit?"

"Yesterday. Paige is NOT happy. I did win that pool, though."

Devon shook his head. "Braedon, I'm in love with Addison."

"Cool. Pretty sure she loves you too, man, but I'll let her tell you that for sure—once we figure out where she is."

"Angie, can you—?"

"Her phone last pinged at South of the Border on I-95. Devon…" Angie looked up from her screen, worry filling her gaze. "It hasn't moved in two days."

"What's she saying?" Braedon asked.

"Hang on, I'm going to put you on speaker." He toggled to speaker and lowered the phone from his face. "Braedon, this is

Angie, our IT guru. She said Addison's phone pinged two days ago at the South of the Border rest stop on I-95."

"I'm familiar with it. There's been nothing since then?"

"No," Angie said. "If she'd kept going, the other towers along I-95 would have picked her up."

"Fuck," Braedon said.

"I'm leaving now," Devon said. "It's two hours north of here."

Paige flew out of her office. "Where's Graham?"

"He's in the conference room, I think," Angie said.

"Get him, now." Angie didn't move fast enough. "Now!"

Angie scrambled up and ran down the hall, the dog chasing after her.

"What's going on?" Braedon asked.

Paige pointed at the phone in his hand. "Who's that?"

"Braedon," Devon said.

"Fuck. My office. Now."

"What's going on?" Braedon asked again.

"I don't know. Hang on a sec." He'd never seen Paige lose her cool. She was the definition of calm, cool, and collected. For her to yell like that, especially at Angie, something bad had happened.

Angie and Graham came down the hall, Angie out of breath. "He's here."

They piled into Paige's office. She turned her computer monitor, revealing Connie on VTC.

"Please repeat what you just told me," she said.

Connie sighed. "Tsarevna escaped the raid on the castle. This video was sent to me late last night. Due to a communications blackout, I only received it thirty minutes ago." She pressed the screen on her phone and held it up to the camera. Tsarevna appeared on her phone screen.

"Constance, you traitorous whore. You will wire ten million dollars to the account I sent to your email to replace the money I would have received from the auction of the two men you stole from me. Don't bother trying to trace where the email came from.

I know these things take time, so you have seventy-two hours to send me the money. If you fail to do so, I will auction off her instead." She stepped to the side, revealing Addison, blindfolded, gagged, and tied to a bed. "I already have many, many people waiting to bid on her."

The video ended, and Connie lowered the phone.

Angie had a hand over her mouth. "Shit," she whispered.

"God damn it," Graham ground out.

"Does she have Addison?" Braedon asked. "Does she have Addison?" he yelled when no one answered him.

"Yes," Devon said.

"Send me the video," Angie said. "And the email."

"Angie—" Connie started.

"I don't care what she said. She doesn't know me. Send me the video and email."

Connie nodded and typed on a keyboard on her desk. "It's on the way."

Angie pushed out of the office.

"Because of the delay, we have less than thirty-seven hours to find her." Connie shook her head. "We won't wire the money. Tatiana knows that. She's just playing with us—with me—as payback."

"We already have a starting point," Devon said. "Addison's phone pinged at a rest stop on I-95 two hours north of here."

"I'll do what I can from my end," Connie said.

"I don't know if she can hear me," Braedon said from Devon's cell phone, "but let her know if she has any kind of authority to keep me from being pulled over, I'm in a dark blue two thousand nineteen Charger. License plate November, zero, tango, delta, echo, delta. See you at South of the Border." He ended the call.

Graham huffed out a laugh. "Got to admire his sense of humor."

"Why?" Paige asked.

Devon smirked. "His license plate says *not dead*."

CHAPTER 26

Oh my God. Why does my head hurt so bad? Addison tried to turn on her side and bury her face in the pillow, but her arms were stuck on something. She pulled on them and felt bindings tighten around her wrists. What the fuck?

She blinked open her eyes and squinted in the light. Was this some weird, kinky game Devon was playing? If it was, why the hell didn't she remember? She racked her brain, trying to remember what led her to being tied to a bed in a dingy motel.

D.C. traffic. Driving to Charleston. She'd been tired so she'd stopped at the obnoxious rest stop just over the South Carolina line. All she needed was coffee and gas. And a chance to gird her loins, so to speak, before the last two hours to Charleston.

Now all she had was a splitting headache and no idea what happened.

A toilet flushed, followed by running water. Should she fake being asleep? Screw that. She yanked on the ropes, wiggling the headboard.

"Oh, good. You're awake. I was worried Andrew had hit you too hard."

What. The. Fuck. Addison stared at Tsarevna as she stood at

the foot of the bed, hands on her hips. Dressed casually in dark jeans and a blouse, with her hair in a low ponytail, she looked different than she had at the castle—almost approachable. Until Addison met her gaze and the familiar derisive gleam in her eyes.

"I see you are surprised to see me," she said. "You almost got me with your little raid, but there are more tunnels under that castle than the one you used."

"You—"

Tsarevna waved a hand. "Yes, yes. I'm not going to get away with this. You have people that will be looking for you. I will pay for this. I've heard it all before. Believe me when I say it never happens the way people think. I always get away with it. No one will find you. And the only person getting paid is me—one way or the other."

She sat in the only chair in the room and crossed her legs. "I will say you surprised me, though. Not too many people are able to do that. I didn't expect you to steal my merchandise."

Addison gnashed her teeth at Braedon and Michael being referred to as merchandise—again. "What did you expect, then?"

"I expected you to bid on your brother to try to win him in the auction." She must have seen the shock on Addison's face. "Oh, yes, I knew who you were almost immediately after you arrived. I always do research on my guests. It was difficult—whoever you work for did a masterful job of scrubbing your online identity, but they missed photos of your brother's funeral."

"Then why play along?" It was very difficult to pull on her wrists without giving away was she was doing.

"Because it amused me. I wanted to watch your face as you realized your brother was so close, only to be ripped out of your grasp. But, like a greedy, entitled American, you decided to take what you didn't possess."

"They're human beings, not possessions."

Any hint of civility fell from Tsarevna's face as she snarled. "They were mine, and you took them." She visibly fought to control her expression. "So I took you. I won't get as much for you as I would have for them, but it will have to do."

The door beeped and opened. Addison strained against the ropes and lifted her head. If someone was outside the room, she could scream for help. She only caught a glimpse of the hood of a car right outside the room before the door closed, but she could hear traffic from the interstate. Were they still at South of the Border?

She recognized the man from the castle. He'd been in the dungeon with them and had followed Tsarevna around like personal security.

"There you are. What took so long? I'm starving." Tsarevna took the bag of to-go containers and set them on the desk. Pulling one out, she opened the lid and grimaced, setting it aside. She did the same with the other two containers.

"What is this slop?"

"It's what they have here," Andrew said.

"I can't eat this. This doesn't even qualify as food."

Addison huffed out a laugh. "What did you expect—gourmet dining? You're at a rest stop in South Carolina with a tower topped with a giant sombrero and a reptile park. Maybe you could try the gator tail. It tastes just like chicken."

Tsarevna sneered. "I'm going to enjoy whipping that attitude out of you before I pass you off."

"I thought she would be let go after you received the money," Andrew said.

"That's what you get for thinking. They are not going to have the money in time and, even if they did, I still would not hand her over. She cost me too much. Lessons must be learned. Now go get me something edible to eat."

Andrew turned toward the door.

"Stop!" Tsarevna stood. "I don't trust you and I'm too hungry for you to figure it out—I'll go myself." She looked at Addison.

"Don't bother testing the ropes. I tied them—you'll never get free until I free you.

"Watch her," she said as she left the room, pulling the door shut with a thud.

Andrew stared out the peephole for several minutes, then moved the curtain aside to watch out the window. Letting it fall, he turned and looked at Addison intently before approaching the bed.

No. Fuck, no. If he came near her, she'd kick him in the face and anywhere else she could reach before she let him rape her. She scooted over as much as she could and turned on her side, kicking out when he got close enough.

"Stop!" he hissed, grabbing her leg.

"No!" She struggled as best she could, wriggling and twisting, kicking and kneeing.

He lay down on top of her and pressed a thumb into the pressure point of her hip.

"Ow!" She jerked her knee up, ineffectually hitting him in the chest.

"If you don't stop struggling, I can't loosen the ropes," he said.

She froze. "What?"

"I can't untie you—she'll realize someone had to let you go and that someone could only be me. I can't afford to lose my cover right now."

"You're—? You're the inside guy?" She didn't want to mention Connie's name in case this was all a ruse.

"Yes. We don't have much time until she figures out there really is nothing to eat here and comes back. Don't kick me when I get off you."

"Okay," she whispered. She still glared at him warily.

He knelt beside the bed and pulled on the frame. "She might have tied you, but I set up the ropes." He yanked on the frame and grunted. "I loosened the frame when I did so it would look like you managed to slip free."

The bed shifted, and he fell back on his ass. "Shit. I thought I'd loosened it more than that."

The rope slackened, and she pulled her arms down, groaning when her muscles protested after being in one position for too long. "How is this going to work? I can't just walk out of here."

He pushed up and helped her sit. "There's a team on the way, but they're about fifteen minutes out. You're going to hit me on the back of the head with the telephone to make it look like you took me by surprise and then you're going to run. There's a cop over by the souvenir shop."

"Where is that from here?"

"It's across the road—we're on the back side of the hotel. There's a bridge that goes over the road if there's too much traffic. Although with your hands tied like that, you might get help faster if you flag someone down."

He unplugged the old-fashioned push-button phone from the wall and handed it to her. "You ready?"

She took the phone and nodded. "Yes."

"Okay. I'm going to kneel on the rug so I don't fall so far."

That surprised a laugh from her. "Okay."

He knelt on the carpet and hung his head down. She lifted the phone over her head and paused.

"You have to do this, Addison."

"Shit. I'm sorry."

"Don't be. I knocked you on the head. It's only fair."

She swung the phone down with all her strength. The bell inside it rang.

He grunted and fell to one elbow, but didn't collapse. "You need to do it harder than that."

She gritted her teeth. With her hands tied together, she wasn't sure she could get the leverage. The decision was taken from her when the lock beeped and the door rattled.

"Shit," she whispered.

Andrew pushed up to one knee. "Give me this." He took the

phone. "Go lie in the bed like you're still tied up. I'll lie in the bathroom like you did knock me out."

"Then what?" she whispered.

"Andrew! The key isn't working. Open the door."

His gaze was heavy. "Do what you have to do."

Addison bit her lower lip and nodded.

Tsarevna banged on the door. "Andrew!"

"Go. Now. She'll figure it out in a second."

He took the phone and lunged into the bathroom, partially closing the door. Addison raced to the bed and gathered the end of the rope in her palms. Raising her arms over her head, she dropped the excess between the mattress and the wall, just as the lock beeped. The tumbler rolled, and the door slammed open.

Her heart pounded in her chest, and she affected what she hoped was a bored expression.

Tsarevna stopped in the doorway and stared at her. "Where is Andrew?"

"Either jacking off or taking a shit."

"What?"

"Bath. Room."

Her nostrils flared, and she slammed the door, throwing the key card on the dresser. "Andrew!"

Addison rolled off the bed as soon as Tsarevna passed the end and reached the corner that led to the bathroom.

"Andrew, so help me…." She pushed the door open. "What—?"

Before she could turn, Addison looped her bound wrists over her head and pulled back, choking her. Tsarevna had at least three inches of height over Addison, more with her heels on, so all Addison had to do was pull her arms in close to her body and let her weight do all the work.

Tsarevna's nails scratched and clawed at Addison's forearms, and blood welled from more than one gouge.

She raised a knee and pushed it into Tsarevna's back. Her knees buckled, and she fell back, taking Addison down with her.

The breath was forced out of her between the hard ground and the weight of Tsarevna on top of her. For one timeless moment, her hold slipped, but Addison twisted her arms again and wrapped her legs around the woman's torso, hooking her feet together.

Tsarevna stopped struggling, and her arms fell limp to her sides.

Addison considered it. God help her, she did. All it would take was one hard twist, and she could break her neck. No one would blame her. She'd been kidnapped. Her brother had been kidnapped and almost trafficked. The woman was the scum of the earth, and she'd be doing the world a favor by killing her.

Just…one…twist.

Glass shattered, and something thudded on the floor.

"Shit!" She pushed Tsarevna off and rolled to her side, curling into a fetal position, pressing one ear into her shoulder and clapping a hand over the other. It had little effect against the percussive blast of the flashbang.

The door bursting open and shouts to get down were muffled by the ringing in her ears. Forcibly hauled up from the ground, she coughed as the cloud from the smoke grenade hit her. Whoever held her dragged her outside and shoved her against the brick wall, pressing on her shoulder to get her to sit.

Addison slid down the wall and rested her head against it, too stunned to do more than sit and watch the tactical team mill about now that the imminent threat had been subdued.

The sound from the activity was muted by the tinnitus caused by the blast. Shaking her head, she stuck a finger in her ear and wiggled it around. Her ears were going to ring for hours.

Connie squatted in front of her. "Sorry we couldn't get here sooner." Her voice was muffled, as if she was speaking to her underwater.

Addison nodded. "That's okay."

"That your handiwork?" She pointed toward the motel room.

Addison nodded.

"She's alive."

She nodded again.

"You had the chance to kill her, but you didn't."

She shook her head slowly.

"How come?"

"I thought about it. I thought about it hard. Before I could decide, you guys threw a flashbang into the room."

Connie shook her head. "You'd already decided. Otherwise she'd be dead." Connie held her gaze, challenging her to argue.

"I didn't want to give her any of my soul."

"It was a good decision," she said.

Addison held up her bound hands. "Can someone cut these off me?"

"Yeah. Hang on a sec." She stopped one of the FBI agents and commandeered his multi-tool, using the saw blade to slice through the ropes.

"So…you work for the FBI?" Addison pulled her wrists apart and shook the remnants off.

Connie grinned and closed the tool. "Something like that."

"Let me through! Let me through!"

They both looked over at the commotion, where three agents were trying to hold Devon back.

"Let him through!" Connie called. She turned back to Addison. "Have EMS look at your wrists before you leave. The FBI will want to debrief you, but I'll work to make that happen quickly."

Devon pushed past the agents and rushed to Addison as she stood up. He grasped her face and kissed her hard. "Fuck. I thought I lost you. I love you. I love you so much."

Joy rushed through her heart in euphoric waves, but she couldn't get the words out. She showed him the only way she could in that moment—by trusting him with her heart. She wrapped her arms tight around him, buried her face in his chest, and cried.

CHAPTER 27

*D*evon pulled the blanket up over Addison's shoulders and brushed a strand of hair out of her face. It had been a long night.

After the doctors ran tests and determined there was no permanent damage to her ears and bandaged her wrists, they'd had to wait for TLC's lawyer to arrive at the hospital so she could sit in on the FBI's questioning. It was technically only a debrief, but since Addison had choked out one of Interpol's most wanted, no one was willing to take any chances. She'd fallen asleep in the car before they ever pulled out of the hospital parking lot.

She hadn't said it back. He'd told her he loved her, but she hadn't given the words back—yet, but it stung. He knew she felt something for him by the way she let him take care of her. It was a lot for a woman like Addison to trust someone and rely on them.

He sighed. Words were just words, but he selfishly wanted them. He eased off the bed and pulled the door closed behind him. In the kitchen, he pulled two long-necks from the fridge and made his way back to the living room, handing one to Braedon.

"Thanks. She still out?"

"Yeah. I think the meds they gave her knocked her out."

"That and she hasn't really been sleeping the last week or so." Braedon sipped his beer and looked at the T.V.

He said it as if it was somehow Devon's fault. Maybe he owed an explanation for why he'd bolted.

"I heard her tell you it was all pretend. That *she* was pretending."

Braedon rolled his head to look at him. "I knew she was lying. Why didn't you? More importantly, why didn't you man up and tell her you weren't pretending?"

"We're gonna do this? Talk about our feelings? You want to turn on the Hallmark Channel afterward?" He knew his bluff wouldn't work, but he needed to buy some time to collect his thoughts.

"It's already on. Spill."

Devon looked at the television. Damned if Jessica Fletcher wasn't sneaking around on screen. He leaned forward and braced his arms on his knees, running a hand over his face. "It stung. My pride. My ego."

"Your heart," Braedon said.

"Yeah. That, too. It was easier to believe the words I heard than trust what I was feeling, so I walked away."

"Look, Addy's been giving me shit about my 'life's too short' philosophy I've got right now, but it is. Bad shit happens, and not just to people like us who go looking for it. Either of you could be hit by a bus tomorrow. Don't waste time walking away from the things that scare you. She might not have said the words yet, but I think she loves you."

Devon swallowed hard. "Why's that?"

"A few reasons. The only person she lets call her Addy is me. Not even our parents call her Addy."

"I call her Addy all the time," Devon said.

Braedon pointed the top of his beer bottle at him. "Exactly."

"Okay, but that doesn't exactly equate to love."

Braedon lowered his beer and stared at the television. "When we were around six, she was crying about something—I don't remember what. Our dad had been drinking and yelled at her to stop crying. I mean, *yelled* at her. She stopped. Immediately. The only person she's cried in front of since then is me." He looked at Devon. "And you. Addy does not trust easily and she doesn't share her feelings—ever—but she does with you."

He turned back to the T.V. "That and the fact she was on her fucking way to tell you how she fucking feels."

Devon looked down and smiled.

"This is a nice house," Braedon said.

"Thanks. I like it."

"It's an old carriage house, right?"

"Yeah."

"Are you renting it?"

Devon shook his head. "No. I bought the property at auction about five years ago. Spent two years renovating this house. I've been working on the big house bit by bit. Eventually, I'll move into the house and rent this out."

Braedon nodded. "Huh."

"Why do you ask?"

"How'd you feel about hiring an inexperienced handyman to help you renovate the house?"

"You getting out?" Devon asked.

"Yeah." He nodded as if not really sure. "Yeah. I am. The Navy's giving me the option to retire, and I'm taking it. I can't keep looking for the bad shit, not after what happened. I can't keep putting Addy and my parents through that. And I figure Addy's going to be spending a lot of time down here in Charleston. It'll be nice to be close to her."

"Uh…how close are we talking?"

Braedon looked him dead in the eye. "I'm going to take the guest room."

Devon pressed his lips together.

Braedon threw his head back, laughing. "Oh, man! You should see your face!" He wiped his eyes. "I'll find an apartment nearby."

Devon's shoulders dropped, and he let out a sigh of relief. Not that he wouldn't enjoy having Braedon around, but not that around.

Still chuckling, Braedon stood and tossed the remote to him. "But right now, I am going to take the guest room because I'm beat. See you in the morning."

"Night." He flipped aimlessly through the channels, hoping something would catch his interest. Finding nothing, he turned off the T.V. and threw his empty bottle in the trash. In the living room, he flipped off the lights and stripped to his boxers. He pulled the back cushions off the couch and tossed them on the chair. Without the cushions, it was almost as wide as a twin bed and comfortable to sleep on—which was one of the reasons he'd bought it. He stretched out, pulling a throw over himself.

Even though they'd slept in the same bed at the castle, after what had happened today, he didn't know how she'd react to waking up in a strange room with someone in bed with her. He'd give her some space for now until they could talk about their future.

～

*D*evon startled awake when the blanket was lifted from his shoulders. Addison lay on the couch and snuggled into his front, pulling the larger blanket from the bed over them.

"Hey," he whispered. "You okay?" From the dim light filtering in through the curtains, it must be around five a.m.

"Yes. Why are you out here?" she asked.

"I didn't want you to wake up in a strange place with a strange man in bed with you."

The corners of her mouth tilted up. "You're not strange. Thank you for coming after me."

"I think Connie got to you first," he said.

"Yeah, but you weren't too far behind."

"I wish I'd gotten there sooner so you didn't have to go through any of it."

"I know." She ran her fingers along his jawline.

He grasped her fingers and kissed them. "I missed you."

"I missed you, too," she said.

"I'm sorry I left Germany without talking to you."

"Why did you?"

"I was in the hall outside Braedon's room and heard you tell him we were only pretending, that none of it was real. It was easier to walk away than face you knowing you didn't feel the same way I did."

"Oh." Addison slid her arm around his waist. "I'm sorry. I lied to him. It wasn't pretend, but we hadn't talked about our feelings or what would happen after the dust settled. I wasn't ready to share the truth with him when I was only coming to terms with it myself. Especially when I wasn't sure you felt the same way."

"So, what's the truth?" His heart thudded against his sternum. He had a good idea what her answer would be, but this was still the second most nerve-racking moment of his life.

"That I'd fallen for you. Hard."

Relief exploded like a starburst, followed quickly by a wave of happiness, and all he wanted was to be as close to Addison as humanly possible. He pressed his mouth to hers and pulled her even closer. Her lips parted, her tongue sliding along his. His cock became rigid and pressed insistently against the front of his shorts.

Rolling her under him, he nestled his hips between her legs and pressed forward. After more than a week apart, it felt like coming home—familiar and comforting.

She groaned and wrapped her outer leg around his lower back, tilting her hips. Her heat permeated through the thin layers of their underwear, stoking his arousal.

A door opened, and someone coughed, then a door closed.

Addison froze and stared at him. "Do you have a roommate?" she whispered.

He shook his head. "It's your brother."

"Braedon's here?" She pushed him off and rolled to her side, facing him again. "We can't have sex if my brother's in the next room."

"Well, that's going to put a damper on things. He's moving in next month."

She stared at him with wide-eyed horror. It must have been similar to the look he'd given Braedon when he'd pulled the same joke on him.

He grinned. "I'm kidding, but he did mention moving down here. He's under the impression you'll be spending a lot of time here."

She bit her lip. "Would you be okay with me moving here?"

He leaned up on an elbow. "Addy, if I had it my way, you'd move in with me tomorrow."

"I think moving in right away would be a mistake. We need to date and get to know each other before we move in together."

"I know everything I need to know about you," he said.

"Really? What if I squeeze my toothpaste from the middle of the tube? What if you leave your toenail clippings on the bathroom counter? What if I like really gross stuff for breakfast, like... like...? I can't think of anything gross right now, but you get the point."

"I know you don't squeeze your toothpaste from the middle. I clip my toenails over the toilet. And as long as you don't eat raw eggs for breakfast, it doesn't matter. But, yes, I get your point. We'll go as fast or as slow as you want."

"I love you," she said.

Relief surged through him, and he pressed his forehead to hers. "That's all *I* want."

"I'm impressed," Braedon said, setting the box marked kitchen on the island. "You made it three whole months before you caved."

Addison glared at her brother. "Shut up, I didn't cave. It was my idea. I was sleeping here all the time anyway."

"You lost me twenty dollars, by the way. I had you holding out for another week."

"Who won?" she asked. Not that she cared. She got a kick out of all the pools Leonidas ran.

"Devon did." He plopped on the couch, stretching his legs out on the ottoman.

"Did he really?"

He stared at her suspiciously. "Did you know what week he bet on? Is that why you agreed to move in?"

She threw her head back and laughed. "No, I didn't know. I didn't even know there was a pool." She tossed a stress ball she found in one of the boxes at his head. "Aren't you supposed to be helping carry in boxes?"

"I did." He pointed at the box he'd carried in.

"One box is not helping. Go help!"

He groaned dramatically but pushed up from the couch. "But I'm retired."

"Just because you retired from the Navy, doesn't mean you qualify for AARP! Go!"

"Fine! You're a horrible sister!"

She grinned after him as he stomped out the door. She loved having him so close. Even though they'd rented an apartment together not far from downtown, she had spent most of her time at Devon's house—now their house. Moving her stuff from the apartment to the carriage house was a technicality.

"How can you have so many boxes of shoes?" Braedon asked, coming back in. "You wore a uniform for thirteen years. Why do you need all these shoes?"

"You realize I didn't wear a uniform twenty-four seven, right?"

"You know Devon's going to kick you right back out when he sees all your shoes."

She rolled her eyes and continued to unpack the box she was working on.

"What am I going to do when I see all her shoes?" Devon set a box on the dining room table. "This is the last one."

"You're going to kick her out when you see all her shoes," Braedon said.

Devon joined her in the kitchen, pressing her back against the counter and threading his hand through the hair at the nape of her neck. "I like her shoes."

She grinned up at him. He always had his hands on her if they were near each other. It surprised her how much she loved it and how often she found herself seeking out his touch.

Wrapping her arms around his waist, she raised her face for a kiss. He didn't disappoint. He never did.

Braedon made gagging sounds, which made her smile even more. Before Devon, she'd never smiled and kissed at the same time.

"I'm interviewing contractors tomorrow," Braedon called.

Devon lifted his head slightly—"Okay"—and went right back to kissing her.

"One of them's a troll. He might demand your first-born as payment."

Devon's shoulders shook as he laughed.

"Okay," she said.

"After that, I'm going to invade a small Caribbean country."

"Make sure it has nice beaches," Devon said.

"I'm going to puke."

"Do that in the neighbor's bushes, please," Addison said.

"You guys are gross. I'm leaving."

"Bye," they both said.

"I'm happy for you, though!"

"Love you, too!" Addison yelled.

The door closed, and they stared at each other, then burst into laughter.

"Now that I've got you moved in how long do I have to wait to talk you into marrying me?" Devon asked.

Her smile felt like it was going to split her face. "That depends."

"On?"

"How big is the pool on when you propose?"

"Well, the pool isn't for when I ask, it's for when you say yes. It was a fifty-dollar buy-in. Last I heard it was five hundred dollars."

"Did you buy in?" she asked.

"They wouldn't let me. Something about insider information."

"Well, someone is going to be very happy tomorrow. Yes."

He froze. "Yes? Really yes? You'll marry me?"

She laughed. "Yes, I'll marry you. Not tomorrow, but I love you and want to spend the rest of my life with you."

"Shit. You know this wasn't really the proposal. I expected you to tell me to try in a few months. I don't even have a ring."

"I don't need a ring, Devon. All I need is you. Although, I do have this, if you can think of something to do with it." She pulled out a length of silk cord from the box on the counter.

Devon pressed her harder against the counter, grinding his erection against her stomach. "God damn, I love you."

That was the only truth she ever needed.

ACKNOWLEDGMENTS

First and foremost, I want to thank the readers, bloggers, and romance lovers who make it possible to keep doing this.

To my fellow WWWW Authors: I love you! I'm so happy we've formed our little tribe.

Finally, my mom and my sister who have been so, SO supportive of this journey. They've encouraged me and pushed me and given me the ability to explore writing full-time. I wouldn't be able to do this without them.

ABOUT THE AUTHOR

Tarina is an award winning author who has spent her entire life in and around the military - first as a dependent and then as an enlisted Air Force member. She uses her life as inspiration for many of her stories, because truth is stranger (and funnier) than fiction.

Tarina is retired Air Force and a single mom of rambunctious twins. Her favorite hobbies are traveling and naps. You can find her trying to find the perfect writing spot with a cup of coffee next to her.

Stay Connected
Website
Email
Newsletter